Number Four: Texas A&M Southwestern Studies

ROBERT A. CALVERT AND LARRY D. HILL
General Editors

Journal of an Indian Trader

Journal of an Indian Trader

Anthony Glass and the Texas

Trading Frontier, 1790–1810

EDITED BY

Dan L. Flores

Texas A&M University Press

College Station

Library of Congress Cataloging in Publication Data

Glass, Anthony, ca. 1773–1819?
   Journal of an Indian trader.

   (Texas A&M southwestern studies; no. 4)
   Bibliography: p.
   Includes index.
   1. Glass, Anthony, ca. 1773–1819?—Diaries.
2. Frontier and pioneer life—Texas. 3. Texas—
Description and travel. 4. Indians of North America—
Texas. 5. Pioneers—Texas—Diaries. 6. Hunters—
Texas—Diaries. 7. Texas—Biography. I. Flores,
Dan L. (Dan Louie), 1948– . II. Title.
III. Series.
F389.G52A33 1985   976.4'02'0924   85-40049

ISBN 0-89096-245-9

Manufactured in the United States of America
FIRST EDITION

This book is dedicated
to the memory of the great natural community
of the early southern prairies

In re-examining the frontier we need to know more about the elusive and flexible frontier trader, his attitudes and his world, for in many instances he was more of a key figure in Indian history than the missionary was.

Howard R. Lamar
The Trader on the
American Frontier

[These Comanches] have great Numbers of Horses and Mules, some of which are Wild Ones Caught by them & domesticated; but they are Mostly rais'd by themselves; Many of them are remarkably fine form'd large Animals, Strongly Mark'd with Arabian features.

John Sibley
October 25, 1807

whoever furnishes Indians the Best & Most Satisfactory Trade can always Control their Politicks.

John Sibley
November 28, 1812

Contents

List of Illustrations

Preface

FULLY a decade before the large-scale entrance of "mountain men" into the Northern Plains and Rockies, American hunters and traders from the southern frontier were penetrating the Comanche plains of present western Oklahoma and West Texas. Contemporaries, even predecessors, of such fabled early Westerners as John Colter, and Wilson Price Hunt and the Overland Astorians, these southern plainsmen were followers and in some cases former associates of Philip Nolan, the Natchez mustanger killed by the Spaniards in 1801. Like their counterparts in the north, most were from river towns on the edge of the settlement line, commonly either Natchez, in the Mississippi Territory, or Natchitoches, the western outpost of the Orleans Territory. Their transportation artery and highway into the hinterland was the line of the Red River, "next to the Missouri, the most interesting water of the Mississippi," Thomas Jefferson had called it, but a river which led them not to the Rockies but to small, detached plains mountains, and to an extensive steppe-plateau. For the most part they followed trails blazed decades before by Pierre ("Pedro") Vial and a host of unnamed French traders.

How many of these American hunter-traders made expeditions into the Southwest between 1790 and 1810 is something we cannot now determine with exact certainty. The expedition led by Anthony Glass seems to be only one of nearly a dozen documented trading forays launched from the southern frontier in the decade after Nolan's death. Glass is among the three or four expedition leaders whose importance transcended prairie trade, for they were recruited as semiofficial emissaries of the United States government, whose presents (often of American flags) and trade were designed to woo the powerful plains tribes away from Spanish allegiance. What separates Glass from the rest is that his 1808–1809 expedition became the first party of whites ever to see Po-a-cat-le-pi-le-car-re ("Medicine Rock"), a huge meteorite venerated as a healing shrine by the Comanches, Taovayas, and other tribes; and more important, the fact that alone among these early southwestern traders, Glass kept a journal detailing his route and experiences.

The present study has been undertaken with a view toward reconstructing, insofar as the scattered extant materials will allow, the dimensions of a frontier whose outlines have been blurred by time and historical neglect. In spite of the attention given Philip Nolan, the early Anglo-American traders of the Southern Plains have not had their historian. Even the Anthony Glass Journal, the most important document of the period and a gem for the study of the American West, has only recently become known. Forgotten for nearly two centuries, portions of it finally were published in 1983 when Elizabeth John's "Portrait of a Wichita Village, 1808," appeared in the *Chronicles of Oklahoma*, and in my study *Jefferson and Southwestern Exploration* (1984). Not until this, however, has the entire Glass document appeared in full with interpretation.

Outside the rich historical broth enveloping it, the Glass Journal cannot properly be appreciated. Of necessity the story is larger than Glass alone, so I have endeavored to interpret the events of the trading frontier of 1790–1810 with broad brush strokes. Even so, the heart of the book remains the annotated Glass journal. Here the student of western history will find not only an intriguing and earthy sketch of the wilderness from which Louisiana, Oklahoma, and Texas were carved, but also the earliest firsthand description by an American of the life of the prairie Taovaya-Wichitas and the plains Comanches. Glass offers, for the Southwest, a raw sketch of the sort John Colter might have left us had he kept a journal. Alone among the documents of the period, it enables us to "accompany" a trading expedition and to catch a fair scent of the experience.

Illustrations to accompany the Glass journal have come primarily from two sources. For purposes of portraying the Indians and the early nineteenth-century life-styles of the Southern Prairies, no gallery or painter surpasses George Catlin's work among the Comanches and "Pani Picts" (Taovaya-Wichitas) in 1834. Catlin's rapid sketches and watercoloring techniques result in images more stylized than those by Friedrich Richard Petri or Seth Eastman, who both portrayed similar Texas subjects two decades after Catlin. But neither Petri nor Eastman, nor even Lino Sánchez y Tapia, who painted Texas Indians in the

1830s, preserved so wide a variety of Indian scenes for us as the inspired Philadelphia lawyer.

Modern photographs of the countryside of the Southern Plains traders' frontier are from my negative files; all of them are from shots made from 1981 to 1984.

I have been working on the Glass project, usually indirectly, as a sideline to other research, for better than a decade, and during that time have incurred many debts. My principal debts to institutions are to the Sterling Memorial Library of Yale University, New Haven, for providing me with a microfilmed copy of the Glass journal and permission to use it; the Watson Memorial Library at Northwestern State University of Louisiana, Natchitoches; the Barker Texas History Center at the University of Texas at Austin; the Mississippi Department of Archives and History, Jackson; the Missouri Historical Society, St. Louis; the Federal Record Center in Fort Worth; and to the Southwest Collection and University Library, Texas Tech University, Lubbock. For their assistance in providing illustrations for the book, I am indebted also to the National Museum of American Art, Smithsonian Institution, Washington; the Peabody Museum of Natural History, Yale University; the Lindenwood Colleges, Saint Charles, Missouri; the Houghton Library, Harvard University; the Walters Art Gallery, Baltimore; the Texas Memorial Museum, Austin; the Gilcrease Institute of History and Art, Tulsa. Many individuals at these libraries and collections have been extremely helpful, but I should particularly mention Carol Wells of Northwestern State and Barbara Narenda of the Peabody Museum.

I am indebted to Elizabeth A. H. John of Austin, Texas, for her help and advice; to Haynes Dugan of Shreveport, Louisiana, for his assistance in procuring documents; to Gabriela Vigo of Lubbock, Texas, for her aid in document translation; to Mrs. Ceress Newell of Spartanburg, South Carolina, for her kindness in sharing with me her genealogical work on the Glass family of Mississippi; and to my brother, Bob Flores, of Mesquite, Texas, who opened my eyes to many fascinating avenues of investigation into history and landscape.

My thanks also to Bob Calvert of the Department of History, Texas A&M University; to Kate Dowdy, who helped me retrace the route of the expedition, and whose photograph of the bois d'arc tree appears here; and to Amy Troyansky, who drew the maps that accompany the book.

One final acknowledgment: I would like to express my deep gratitude to Ms. Katherine Bridges of Amarillo, Texas, former archivist at the old "Louisiana Room" at Northwestern State University in Natchitoches, for introducing me more than a decade ago to Anthony Glass, John Sibley, Freeman and Custis, and to the range of documents from which the history of the Louisiana-Texas frontier must be written. Although not the book she could have produced, this study, it is hoped, will merit her approval.

Dan L. Flores
Yellow House Canyon, Texas
February, 1984

PART 1
Introduction

The American Trader and the
Southwestern Frontier

We crossed the Mississippi on the 1st day of November, 1800, at
the Walnut Hills, and in January following arrived at the river
Brassus, in the province of Texas, and proceeded to build pens. In
March 1801, we began to run wild horses. . . . On the 22d of
March, we were attack[ed] at break of day. . . . Our commander
(Nolan) being killed, we capitulated in the evening. . . .[1]

IN the summer of 1807, more than six years after the incarceration
of twelve Americans in the prisons of New Spain, explorer Zebulon
Montgomery Pike penned a letter to the Natchez *Herald* relating the
situation of "the poor unfortunate companions of the deceased [Philip]
Nolan."[2] Himself a "captive" of Spanish officials for several months,
Pike was in a sound position to warn Americans on the southwestern
frontier of the dangers of trespass into Spanish dominions. To Philip
Nolan's friends and potential imitators in Natchez, Natchitoches, and on
the hardscrabble wilderness farms around them, the message must
have been plain: despite the easy wealth in hides, honey, and wild
horses that beckoned from the prairies of Texas, Spain continued to
hold the province, and to regard all American incursions as threats to
her territorial integrity. And, seemingly, neither President Jefferson's
claim that Texas was part of the Louisiana Purchase, nor the near war
following the stopping of his Red River exploring party by a Spanish
army, had changed that basic policy.

The early American frontier of the old Southwest has never received the historical attention lavished upon the Missouri River and
the Northern Plains and Rockies of the beginning decades of the nineteenth century. Perhaps the romance associated with Lewis and Clark
and the mountain men who followed them has been responsible. Whatever the reason, with the exceptions of the Pike expedition and the forays of Philip Nolan, most of the details of the early American thrust
into the Southwest are imperfectly known and understood, at least until the time of American filibustering in the Mexican Revolution, and

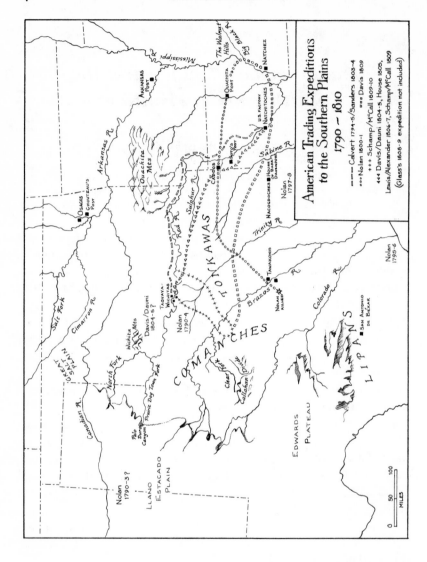

American Trading Expeditions
to the Southern Plains
1790 ~ 1810

- - - Calvert 1794-5/Sanders 1803-4
ooo Nolan 1800-1   □□□ Davis 1809
+++ Schamp/McCall 1809-10
⌁⌁⌁ Davis/Dauni 1804-5, House 1805,
Lewis/Alexander 1806-7, Schamp/McCall 1809
(Glass's 1808-9 expedition not included)

the advent of the Santa Fe trade in 1821.[3] Nevertheless, the Louisiana-Texas frontier during the two decades prior to the outbreak of the revolution in Mexico (or, from 1790 to 1810) was an important front of American penetration into the West. The principal actors on this front composed a cast only slightly different from that in the more familiar north: Jeffersonian explorers, powerful Western Indian nations, and strong-willed Indian agents, were common to both frontiers; we need substitute only Spanish officials for British ones, traders for trappers, and (in terms of wilderness booty), wild horses and bison robes for beaver.

The focus of this study is on the American traders, long maligned in historical scrutiny of the West. Only recently have modern interpretations portrayed the traders more sympathetically. Howard R. Lamar, for example, recently has characterized the frontier trader as a prototype entrepreneur who lived "in a fascinating world which combined the hunting-scavenging lifestyle with mercantile capitalism."[4] A major reason for this diversity of scholarly opinion has been, in fact, the paucity of primary material on the traders.

As a consequence of the spirited Spanish resistance to Jefferson's government exploring party, even more so than the mountain men of the north these traders on the southwestern plains tended to become instruments of United States expansionist policy towards the West. In the struggle between Spain and the United States over where the boundary between Louisiana and Texas would be drawn, for several years war loomed as a distinct possibility. Critical in such a conflict, as well as in the general imperial struggle, were the allegiances of the Indian nations of the interior, particularly those powerful and numerous tribes separating the Americans from New Mexico and Santa Fe.

Among these *norteños*, as the Spaniards called them, the most important were the numerous and powerful Comanche bands, and their allies, the Wichitan peoples of the upper Brazos and Red River country. Particularly critical were the three Red River villages (the "master-key of the north") occupied primarily by Taovayas and Wichitas, but also by Iscanis and, often, Skidis (the latter famous for their obsession with astronomy and for producing "star cult" shamans).[5] These groups were precisely the tribes Spain found most difficult to manipulate from her garrisons in San Antonio and Nacogdoches and whose historic trade ties, particularly for the Red River villages, had

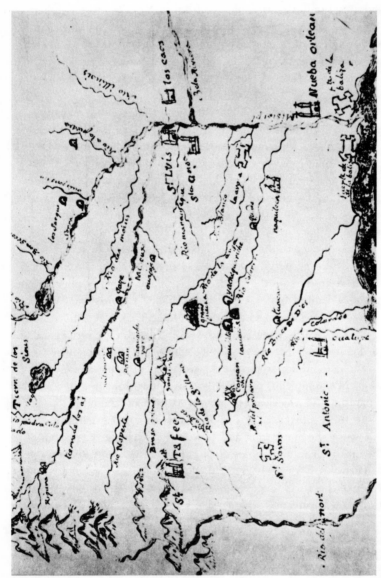

Pierre ("Pedro") Vial's 1787 manuscript map gave Spanish frontier authorities an amazingly accurate knowledge of western geography and emphasized the key location of the Taovaya-Wichita villages on the Red River. (From Carl I. Wheat, *Mapping the Transmississippi West*)

Map of the Louisiana-Texas Frontier, ca. 1804, from information compiled by General James Wilkinson largely from Philip Nolan's trading-mustanging forays. The map appears here slightly cropped. (Courtesy Houghton Library, Harvard University)

been to the French at Natchitoches and the Arkansas Post. They also possessed the greatest numbers of horses and mules of any tribes in the West, a fact that was not lost on would-be American traders living on the frontier. Thus did the objectives of private American traders and their government complement one another in the Southwest.

Just as the Americans inherited the French side of the century-old struggle for tribal allegiance, so too the frontier traders found themselves involved in a trade whose origins were at least half a century old. Thanks to work done by Francis Haines and J. Frank Dobie, most of the details of the diffusion of Spanish horses throughout the West have now been known for four decades.[6] From the Santa Fe and Taos settlements, tribes of the Mountain West were acquiring both horse and the cultural complex of its use by the middle of the seventeenth century. By 1690, when Henri de Tonty was among the Caddos on the Great Bend of the Red River, they too possessed some thirty riding horses.[7] Spanish efforts between 1690 and 1720 to block the French advance brought hundreds of animals, both mares and stallions, into Texas, many of which escaped and became feral.[8] By 1705 notices of these "wild" animals begin to appear in the Spanish documents.

The wild horses of the early West were descendants of Andalusian stock, a line of animals whose ancestry can be traced to the Barbary and Arabian horses of northern Africa and the Middle East. Small, fleet, and often beautifully proportioned, these animals were ideally shaped by their desert evolution to compete as grazers with bison and pronghorn antelope on the prairies and plains of the Southwest. By 1800 they had reached a peak population of perhaps two million, most between the Rio Grande and the Arkansas rivers, the center of their range, apparently, west-central Texas. Although difficult to catch, since they were feral (rather than truly wild) animals they were fairly easy to tame, and by the 1770s hundreds of them were being driven east, along with horses raised or stolen by the plains tribes, to supply American farmers of the trans-Appalachian frontier with inexpensive work and riding stock. Natchez and Saint Louis became the principal centers of distribution for unbroken mustangs, ordinary specimens of which brought ten to twenty dollars, and the Chickasaw and Osage peoples, respectively, the middlemen of the trade.[9]

Anglo-Americans along the southern frontier took cognizance of the possibilities Texas offered long before the great purchase of 1803.

In the period from 1790 to 1810 there were perhaps two million wild mustangs between the Rio Grande and Arkansas rivers. (George Catlin, courtesy National Museum of American Art, Smithsonian Institution)

Natchez on the Mississippi (ca. 1800), the "Saint Louis" of the southwestern frontier. (Courtesy Mississippi Department of Archives and History)

Between 1783 and 1798 (the year the boundary established by the Pinckney Treaty of 1795 was drawn), Natchez lay within territory claimed by the United States but governed by Spain as a part of West Florida.[10] During the period the surrounding area filled with Americans, Scots, and Irish, who watched as thousands of horses were brought into West Florida from Texas. Among these was a young native of Belfast who was raised—in a relationship that has never been explained—in the home of American general James Wilkinson. His name was Philip Nolan.

Philip Nolan and Texas

Philip Nolan is a legendary figure in Texas history. While most of the details of his story have already been pieced together, most recently (and expertly) by Noel Loomis,[11] the general outline is so crucial to this study we must reexamine it here. To subsequent traders like Anthony Glass, Nolan undoubtedly was both example and apotheosis.

The transcendent image left by the documents is of a literate, athletic, and adventurous young man, confident in his wide-ranging talents. William Dunbar, who directed Jefferson's southwestern exploring probes (leading one himself) and was skilled in evaluating men, thought Nolan lacked a sufficient education and was flawed by eccentricities "many and great." Nevertheless, he told Jefferson, Nolan "was not destitute of romantic principles of honor united to the highest personal courage," and he possessed an energy "which under the guidance of a little more prudence might have conducted him to enterprises of the first magnitude." Nolan's friend, Daniel Clark, Jr., of New Orleans, regarded him, less critically and more simply, as an "extraordinary Character," one "whom Nature seems to have formed for Enterprises of which the rest of Mankind are incapable."[12]

He was barely twenty when, in 1790, he petitioned Louisiana governor Esteban Miró for a passport and planned his first trip into Texas. For the better part of the next two years he evidently explored the upper Red River and New Mexico in company with the Taovaya-Wichitas and the Comanches, providing those peoples with an initial, highly favorable impression of the Anglo-American. Nolan seems also to have been the first Mississippian to discover the possibilities of a trading connection with these bands—an arrangement the Indians no doubt promoted. In an effort to regulate more carefully *norteño* trade, Spanish officials had abolished the historic trade tie with Natchitoches in favor of a more strictly supervised overland exchange with San Antonio and Nacogdoches—by the late 1790s increasingly with the trading house of William Barr, Edward Murphy, and Samuel Davenport in the latter settlement. Permitted to secure American, British, and French manufactured goods in Louisiana for the Texas Indians, these naturalized Spaniards augmented the supply of goods available from Mexico City, and were allowed to exploit the mustang trade of the plains. But the Taovaya-Wichitas and southern Comanches were unhappy with the arrangement, for it more severely restricted their access to guns, traditionally available from Natchitoches since the days of the French; Spanish officials sought to control gun trafficking because it undermined the long-standing policy of discouraging Indians from the chase and raiding. This became a situation under which the Red River tribes chafed, particularly as their enemies, the Osages, were not only well armed themselves, but were effectively preventing traders from Saint Louis and the Arkansas Post from bringing guns into the country farther west. Philip Nolan's brief second trip into Texas in 1794 may have been designed to help alleviate the situation. He says only that he "turned hunter; sold skins," but he early on acquired a source of trade guns, for by 1797 he would even offer to outfit Spanish troops with muskets he could deliver to San Antonio "for eighteen pesos each, equal in their workmanship to the best in use by the troops of your excellency."[13] However he acquired them, in 1794 he made his way back to Natchez with fifty mustangs to sell.

He had found "the savage life . . . less pleasing in practice than speculation" (he could not "Indianfy my heart" as he put it),[14] but in January of 1796 he returned from a third trading-mustanging foray. He was getting considerably better at it by now. This time he had 250 horses, several of which he decided to take to Frankfort, Kentucky, to sell—an activity that brought him and his horses to the attention of important people. On the third trip he had explored what he called "the unknown land" along the Texas coast to Laredo, and inland to San Antonio and Chihuahua.

By 1797 Nolan possessed more information about Texas than almost anyone on the frontier, and both Americans and Spaniards were coming to realize it. Spanish officials began to turn against him following his meeting with Andrew Ellicott, the American commissioner and chief surveyor for the West Florida boundary settlement.[15] Louisiana governor Baron de Carondelet granted Nolan still another passport, but by the fourth trip Nolan's talents clearly were being used to American advantage. Thus he wrote to James Wilkinson: "I have instruments to enable me to make a more correct map than the one you saw; Ellicott assisted me in acquiring a more perfect knowledge of astronomy and glasses; and Gayoso himself made me a present of a portable sextant. My timepiece is good. I shall pay every attention, and take an assistant with me, who is a tolerable mathematician."[16]

He set out on the fourth expedition in July of 1797, with "twelve good rifles, and . . . but one coward," packing seven thousand dollars worth of goods. A year later the party returned with twenty-five hundred horses, most traded for from the Indians, some fifteen hundred of which they left temporarily in Nacogdoches. At some point following this fourth expedition Nolan sketched (or provided information for) a series of maps—very likely the same maps Wilkinson showed to Aaron Burr in May of 1804 and sent to U.S. Secretary of War Henry Dearborn the following July.

One of the so-called "Burr maps" which has survived is a handsomely done, untitled representation of the Louisiana-Texas frontier, supposed to have been among Burr's possessions when he was captured early in 1807. Probably drafted from manuscript charts in the year 1804, this map is an invaluable document, one which demonstrates a sound American knowledge of the Texas frontier at the time of the Louisiana Purchase. It accurately locates virtually every Indian nation of the border country and provides detailed but fragmentary information on settlements, harbors, and rivers. Wilderness specifics are limited, perhaps because the upper Red River is not portrayed. Pieces of the Cross Timbers and a "Salt River" (probably the Little Wichita) do appear, but except for the inscription "Great Plains" across north Texas, and one designating the "Winter hunting grounds of the Cumanches or Hyatans" on the Colorado, the plains are left terra incognita. The map unquestionably is authentic and certainly is one of the maps which Wilkinson had made, from information gathered primarily by Philip Nolan, for Burr and the government in the spring of 1804.[17]

Through Wilkinson, Nolan seems also to have left us a verbal description of the Southwest, particularly of the wild country beyond the headwaters of the Red River, that expresses the southern traders' image of the West. While men of science and officials of two governments indulged in fantasies about the area and its rivers, Nolan knew the country firsthand and honestly. Beyond the Taovaya-Wichita villages, farther out on the prairies, the traders knew that the Red River forked, and that the North Fork flowed through "a Ridge of mountains" (now the Wichita and Quartz Mountains). The longer fork was the "left branch" (Prairie Dog Town Fork), which took its source, "in the East side of a height, the top of which presents an open plain, so extensive as to require the Indians four days in crossing it, and so destitute of water, as to oblige them to transport their drink in the preserved entrails of beasts of the Forest."

On the other side of this "high plain" there was a river running south and beyond it "a ridge of high mountains extending North and South." That is as good a geographical rendering of the Llano Estacado–Pecos River–Sangre de Cristo Mountains country as one is likely to find.[18]

During his absence in 1798, Nolan had received a most important letter. Vice-president Thomas Jefferson, hearing of Nolan through Wilkinson and Senator Brown of Kentucky, had written to him that summer, requesting natural-history data on the southwestern mustangs at "the only moment in the age of the world" when the horse could "be studied in its wild state." By early 1800 Jefferson was expressing a desire to purchase one of Nolan's animals, "which I am told are so remarkable for the singularity & beauty of their colours & forms." According to both Wilkinson and Daniel Clark, this led "the Mexican traveller" and an "Inhabitant of the western Country" (a specialist in Indian sign language) to depart for Virginia in May of 1800, taking with them a fine paint stallion for Jefferson. For some reason Nolan got no farther than Kentucky. The historical evidence in the Jefferson Papers is clear that Nolan, apparently anxious to return again to Texas, stood up the man about to be elected president.[19]

Now convinced that Nolan had "a commission from General Wilkinson to make an expert reconnaissance of the country,"[20] Spanish officials set in motion an effort to stop another expedition. By October of 1800, however, Nolan wrote Jesse Cook in Nacogdoches that he was embarking upon a fifth foray: "I am taking a large quantity of goods. Everyone thinks that I go to catch wild horses, but you know that I

The Red River took traders not to the Rockies but to the Wichita ranges, as seen here from the North Fork of the Red.

have long been tired of wild horses. . . . I have good men and never will be taken. . . . I know the coast so well between Opelousas and River Grand that it will be difficult to overtake or attack me." Actually, Nolan had only three packhorses worth of trade goods this trip. But he had nearly two dozen men, armed to the teeth, and himself carried a saber, four pistols, and two carbines. According to one report, he also was carrying mining tools with him. In 1800, however, he had no passport. Eighteen-year-old Ellis Bean's version of the trip was that the party left the Walnut Hills in early November and by December had reached the big, open prairies beyond the Middle Trinity. After an excursion northwesterly to a Comanche camp on one of the southern affluents of the Red River, they returned to the mustanging country of central Texas, where Nolan's fate awaited him.[21]

Noel Loomis has argued that Nolan made this last expedition either because he was in love with fifty-year-old Gertrudes de los Santos in Nacogdoches, or because he was involved in one of James Wilkinson's schemes to revolutionize and conquer Texas. Nolan's allegiance, I would argue, lay far more with the latter than the former. The Spaniards were most suspicious, and Texas governor Juan Bautista de Elguezabal decided to dispatch from Nacogdoches Lieutenant Miguel Musquiz and 120 troops to "arrest" Nolan. On March 21, 1801, Tawakoni scouts located Nolan's camp, in the Grand Prairie, near today's Nolan's Branch of the Brazos. In midmorning a wild shot took Nolan full in the forehead. Seven of Nolan's men escaped, including Robert Ashley and John House, both of Natchez. As we have seen, there were still twelve Americans from the party languishing in Spanish jails as late as 1807.

Traders to the Plains

Behind the Spanish wish to end Nolan's liberties in their provinces was a fear that Nolan might set a precedent for other Americans to follow. For two or three years, the Nolan episode does indeed seem to have caused American enthusiasm for Texas to ebb somewhat. By April of 1804, however, when Capt. Edward D. Turner took possession of Natchitoches, the most westerly of the new American outposts in the Louisiana Purchase, those frontier hunter-traders who found the stories told of the "Great Plains" irresistible, once again began to probe at Texas. These men, many of them Philip Nolan's friends and all of them his followers, found themselves recruited even more actively to serve American policy vis-a-vis the Southwest.

Just who were these southern hunter-traders who, in the face of very real dangers, were so anxious to venture onto the Comanche plains? The common image of the frontier trader is in sharp contrast to that of the mountain trapper. Traders are traditionally treated as "dispicable characters cavorting with Indians and supplying them with guns,"[22] rather than as wilderness heroes. Lewis O. Saum, in *The Fur Trader and the Indian*, has argued that there were actually two classes of traders on the frontier. One, the licensed traders and expedition leaders, were usually middle-class men of substance and character. They possessed some capital to underwrite their ventures, and commonly they were literate.[23] These were the "Booshways" (bourgeoise) of the mountain trade, men like William Ashley and Milton Sublette. On the Southern Plains a decade earlier they were people like Philip Nolan and Anthony Glass.

The second group ("independent and unlicensed," Saum charac-

terizes them) eventually became the backbone of the "free" trappers of
the mountains, and they filled in the ranks of the early trading expeditions launched from the southern frontier. The picture of them that
emerges from the documents is one of young men from the squatters'
farms on the edge of the frontier, whose chief skill was hunting, and
whose motivation was as much wanderlust as pecuniary gain. They were
men of action rather than words, and most of them were illiterate.[24] But
they knew guns and Indians, and how to exist in the wilderness.

John Maley, himself an itinerant wanderer who evidently visited
the southern frontier, was not flattering in his appraisal of the Red
River hunters he met:

> Their are a great number of hunters here [Natchitoches] that go up a great
> distance in order to kill bufaloe and hunt bees. They only bring down the bee's
> wax, bufaloe tallow, and their tongues dried. The carcase and skin is thrown to
> the vermin. What a vast destruction here is only for the benefit of a few
> straglers who in such a country as this might be a publick good and also a good
> to themselves, where now they are and entire nuisance. When they come to
> market with their produce they never return untill they have spent all they
> made in the season before. It is necessity that compells them to retire to the
> woods there to live like Indians and also commit depredations on the natives.
> If they come across their encampment [these hunters] will plunder them of all
> their property which causes those friendly nations to become hostile and have
> reason to suspect every honest trader that should wish to venture among them
> and also get a general information of the country, which from such men we
> cannot get with any accuracy. They should wish it never to be known in their
> time.[25]

Maley clearly is describing the worst of them, but this is the genus
of men who not only cleared the beaver from the Rockies but also
manned the early American thrusts at the Spanish Southwest.

Possibly the earliest Anglo-American not associated with Nolan to
penetrate into the Southern Plains was one "Juan Chalvert," a Philadelphia Presbyterian whose name must actually have been John Calvert. A gunsmith by trade, in 1794—at age 27—Calvert made his way
up the Red River to the Taovaya-Wichita villages, where he was welcomed for his skills, and where he lived with an Indian girl who bore
him a son. For fourteen months the young Philadelphian lived with the
Indians, hunting bison and mustangs and repairing their guns, before
being arrested (1795) by a Spanish patrol and taken to Coahuila.[26]

Although there must have been others, an American hunter named Sanders is the first trader in the post-Nolan period known to have attempted a similar feat. Sanders's precise identity is unknown. In the autumn of 1803, however, he is reported to have ascended the Red River (the document implies water travel) to the Taovaya-Wichita villages, finding them eager for trade with the Americans. Sanders was chased by a Spanish patrol, but arrived safely in Natchitoches in July of 1804.[27]

Spanish officials in the Provincias Internas (the administrative provinces of northern Mexico, which included New Mexico and Texas) were more alarmed over reports that Robert Ashley of Natchez planned on making an expedition to the Taovaya-Wichitas that winter, to secure supplies of meat and trade for horses. An interesting man in his own right, related by marriage to George Rogers and William Clark, Ashley had come to Natchez from South Carolina in the 1790s. Under Spanish interrogation in 1795, he had admitted that the older Clark had offered him a captaincy in the force that citizen Edmund Genet had tried to raise to invade Spanish possessions.[28] Ashley was a man to be feared, as well, from his earlier association with Nolan, and once again Spanish officials ordered out Miguel Musquiz, this time with 152 men, to pursue Ashley's company. Musquiz nearly caught Sanders in the process, but when he returned in April of 1804 the four months he had spent searching for the Natchez party had been fruitless. Apparently learning of the Spanish reaction, Ashley had cancelled his expedition.[29]

Within six weeks of Musquiz's return, Nacogdoches commandant José Joaquin Ugarte heard that a smaller expedition from Natchitoches (variously reported as totaling either five or seven men) led by "Juan" Davis, one of the most active wilderness traders on the southwestern frontier, and Alexandro Dauni, a Corsican carpenter, had passed through the Caddo village (located on modern Jeems Bayou) en route overland to the Taovaya-Wichita villages.[30] This group was evidently more interested in mines and prospecting than in trade. Although they passed the winter of 1804–1805 with the Taovayas and constructed a cabin, the Indians reported that they spent most of their time farther upriver (ascending the North Fork to the Wichita Mountains?) where they were said to have collected numerous specimens of silver ore. At some point during the winter the Osages had attacked the cabin, kill-

ing one (some reports say three) of them. A command under Lieutenant José Ygnacio Ybarbo was sent in pursuit of the Davis-Dauni party,
but to no effect.[31]

Dr. John Sibley

The most important development on the American side of the border
that autumn of 1804 was the appointment of Dr. John Sibley as "occasional" Indian agent for the United States. Coupled with a congres-
sional appropriation of three thousand dollars for Sibley's use in pur-
chasing presents and trade goods for the Indians of the Southwest, the
United States had, in effect, thrown down the gauntlet to Spain in con-
test for diplomatic alliance with the tribes south of the Arkansas.

Sibley was one of Jefferson's more fortunate civil servant discoveries. At the time of his appointment he was forty-seven, a native of
Massachusetts who had come to Natchitoches in 1803, seemingly in an
effort to escape his second wife in North Carolina (he was periodically
hounded by rumors, which even reached the newspapers, that he was
a "wife-deserter"). Following the submission to Jefferson of his "Historical Sketches" of the tribes of the Southwest, and an account of the Red
River based primarily upon his conversations with François Grappe
and Jean Brevel, a pair of aging French hunter-traders, he was given a
full-time appointment (1805). While he was a master of self-promotion
and not incapable of providing faulty information, he was interested in
and closely observant of Indians and became a tireless promoter of
American interests among them. Orleans Territorial Gov. W. C. C.
Claiborne was responsible for acquainting Jefferson with him, and as
was often true of Jefferson's friendship, the relationship brought out the
best in Sibley. He easily ranks alongside William Clark and Auguste P.
Chouteau as the most influential American contacts with the tribes of
the West during the decade immediately following the great purchase.[32]

The Spanish fear that Sibley was "a revolutionist, the friend of
change" (as Provincias Internas commandant Nemecio Salcedo's widely
quoted remark put it) was not long being confirmed. Adhering to the
Jeffersonian interpretation of the extent of Louisiana and cognizant of
strong interest by the Texas tribes in the Americans, Sibley took advantage of every opportunity to enlarge the American sphere of influence
radiating from Natchitoches. He first made friends with Dehahuit, son

Dr. John Sibley, Natchitoches Indian agent who shaped American diplomacy towards the Southern Plains tribes. (Courtesy Lindenwood Colleges)

of Tinhioüen "the Peacemaker" of the eighteenth century, and the last
of the great Kadohadacho (Caddo) chiefs to rule his people in their ancient homeland.[33] Perhaps no more influential Indian existed in the
near Southwest of that day. The Kadohadachos, linguistically related to
almost all the surrounding tribes (including the Taovayas, Wichitas,
Tawakonis, and other prairie Caddoans), were widely regarded as liai-
sons with the whites and despite a severe, disease-induced decline,
were still considered by most Texas tribes as an ancient and wise
people. Dehahuit's friendship was indispensable to Sibley.

Sibley sent his "first messenger," as the Indians called him, to the
plains tribes in the spring of 1805. In the middle of March, John
House, another of the escaped members of Nolan's ill-fated 1801 expedition, asked Natchitoches officials for a license to trade for horses with
the Indians and to "go hunting up the Natchitoches River." On behalf
of the United States, Sibley sent presents by House to the Taovaya-
Wichitas, Tawakonis, and Comanches, and asked him to urge the Indians to pay a visit to Natchitoches. Early that May Spanish spies reported that a Kichai Indian was guiding the seven-man House expedition to the Taovaya-Wichitas. When new Texas governor Antonio
Cordero y Bustamante talked with Aricara, a subchief of the Tawakonis
six months later, the Indian confirmed that House had been among
them, and that some Texas Indians had already gone to Natchitoches
and had received presents and an American flag. Cordero further
learned that the Americans were providing what, by law and long-
standing custom, Spanish traders could not: guns and powder.[34]

Jefferson's Exploration

In the meantime, an American threat of a more official and far more
serious nature was brewing in Washington and Natchez. President
Jefferson's plan for exploring Louisiana seems always to have included a
second great expedition to be aimed at the southernmost rivers of
the Mississippi drainage, the Red River and the Arkansas River. Portentously, James Wilkinson had already approached Aaron Burr with
his scheme to revolutionize Texas and Mexico when, in the late spring
of 1804, he learned of Jefferson's plans for a southern exploration.
Wilkinson, of course, had regularly provided Spain with American state

secrets since the 1790s, and he quickly relayed this one to his Spanish contacts. Evidently Wilkinson believed that he could foster a war between the two governments over the exploration, then use the hostilities as an excuse for launching a two-pronged invasion of Spanish possessions, led by Burr and himself. While the president and William Dunbar of Natchez were busy screening candidates for field leaders of the expedition, every level of Spanish bureaucracy was buzzing with the news that Jefferson was "invading" the Provincias Internas with a scientific party that planned to penetrate all the way to Santa Fe.[35]

For a multitude of reasons, primarily the administration's difficulty in finding a capable leader who could perform the precision mapwork so necessary to an examination of southern Louisiana, the exploration was delayed for nearly two years. But finally, in the autumn and winter of 1805–1806, Jefferson decided on civil engineer Thomas Freeman as field leader, and after unsuccessfully approaching the aging William Bartram, gave the lucrative appointment of naturalist (for which both Constantine Samuel Rafinesque and Alexander Wilson applied) to young Peter Custis, a medical student studying under Benjamin Smith Barton at the University of Pennsylvania. As commander of the forty-five man military escort, Jefferson insisted on Capt. Richard Sparks, "one of the best woodsmen, bush fighters, & hunters in the army."[36]

At a private White House dinner with Freeman in November of 1805, Jefferson outlined his objectives for the probe, and presented Freeman with a classic, seven-page letter of exploring instructions— one originally drawn up in 1804. Taking frequent observations so as to establish its true course, Freeman's party was to ascend the Red River to its headwaters, believed at that time—in part because of Sibley's testimony—to lie in "the tops of the mountains" near Santa Fe.

Relative to the Indians, Jefferson's intent was unmistakable:

> Court an interview with the natives as intensively as you can . . . make them acquainted with the position, intent, character peaceable and commercial dispositions of the US. inform them that their late fathers the Spaniards have agreed to withdraw all their troops from the Mississippi and Missouri and from all the countries watered by any rivers running into them; that they have delivered to us all their subjects . . . that henceforth we become their fathers and friends that our first wish will be to be neighborly, friendly and useful to them and especially to carry on commerce with them on terms more reasonable and advantageous to them than any other nation ever did.[37]

The expedition not only carried presents and American flags for the tribes of the interior, it also intended on constructing a temporary post among the Taovayas (from whom horses were to be purchased for the final leg of the journey), and using those Indians as intermediaries for treating with the Comanche hordes which, so Sibley said, controlled all the country from the Trinity to the Missouri, and westward past the Rockies.[38]

As details concerning Jefferson's exploration leaked through Wilkinson's agents to Spanish officials in the Provincias Internas, Spain took vigorous action. The threat of an American expedition in territory and among tribes still regarded as subject was exacerbated in February, 1806, with Captain Turner's forceful expulsion of the century-old Spanish command at Los Adaes, east of the Sabine River. More than 540 additional troops were marched into Texas in the spring of 1806, and they were accompanied by the arrival of Salcedo, from Chihuahua, and Col. Simón de Herrera, stellar officer and governor of the state of Nuevo León. "This expedition seems to have thrown their whole Country into commotion," Custis wrote Dearborn, and he did not exaggerate. Two large military expeditions, one of 212 men commanded by Captain Francisco Viana, the new, ramrod-straight commandant at Nacogdoches, and a 600-man force from Santa Fe under Lieutenant Facundo Melgares, were dispatched in June of 1806 to block the American ascent of the river.[39] On July 28, just east of the present border of Oklahoma, the Viana force confronted the 50-man American expedition. Having ascended the Red River for four months and 615 miles, Jefferson's southwestern exploration was forced to abort only halfway to the headwaters, and still three weeks short of the Taovaya-Wichitas and Comanche country. Pike had just left Saint Louis for the West.

There followed, in the posturing of Herrera's force of some 700 and Wilkinson's command of more than 1200, a very tense situation that took the two countries to the brink of war. Fortunately for Spain, rather than prosecute a battle and follow through with the "Burr" conspiracy—Burr at that very moment descending the Mississippi—Wilkinson flinched from the task, proclaiming Burr a traitor who sought to "divide the union," and signed an agreement with Herrera establishing the famous Neutral Ground. All mention of the Red River was omitted from this document, however, and while the ultimate settlement of the boundary was left to the diplomats, the issue of *nor-*

teño allegiance was left open for action.[40] And Pike's inability to find either the Comanches or the headwaters of the Red River before being himself captured early in 1807, had eliminated the last official explorer from the field.

The Lewis and Alexander Expedition

For a Spanish government preoccupied with Napoleon's machinations at home, it had been a close call. Determined now to avoid "any noisy disturbances which might create new cause for friction between the two govnts.," Salcedo and Cordero decided on a new policy respecting American traders among the Texas Indians. Louisiana Indian trader Marcel Soto was instructed to found a new Spanish trading post at Bayou Pierre (south of present Shreveport, and the only post Spain now retained east of the Sabine) to siphon off Indian interest in Natchitoches. More important, the two Spanish leaders decided that from henceforth Indians (rather than the American traders themselves) who were guilty of consorting with the Sibley men were to be punished and deprived of Spanish trade.[41]

This was obviously not a wise policy, and it was put to an immediate test. In the autumn of 1806, in the middle of the crisis, Sibley licensed a trading party led by John S. Lewis and William C. Alexander and guided by Joseph Lucas, a métis interpreter who had accompanied Freeman and Custis and quite possibly was Nolan's sign-language expert, to trade with and take an American flag to the Taovayas. Jeremiah Downs, John Litton, Berimon Watkins, and one Lusk completed the party, which was further instructed to invite the Taovaya-Wichitas, Comanches, and surrounding Indians into Natchitoches for a conference with Sibley the next summer.[42] The Spanish suspicion that these traders were "operating for the gov't. of the U.S." was exactly correct.[43] The diplomatic ends the administration had been unable to accomplish with the western Indians by a government expedition, it seemed determined to effect through the expeditions of private traders.[44]

In June of 1807, Lewis, Downs, and Watkins, herding a drove of mustangs and accompanied by eight Taovayas warriors, returned from their eight-month visit among the upper Red River tribes, leaving Alexander and the others behind to have a final try at catching wild horses. They had gone upriver with few trade goods, but nonetheless

they had been treated graciously by the great Taovayas chief, Awahakei. Lewis reported that during their stay the Taovaya-Wichitas had
been invited to San Antonio by Cordero and the groups that had gone
had returned loaded down with presents. Cordero had also provided
three Spanish flags for their villages, but (according to Lewis) Awahakei
would fly only the American flag they had brought him, and sent word
that he wanted flags for each of the other villages. The traders had
been invited to visit a Comanche camp forty miles from the Taovaya-
Wichitas that contained some three thousand people and five thousand
horses and mules. Per Sibley's instructions, Lewis had summoned its
chiefs and leading men to Natchitoches. Lewis told Sibley that the
country over which they had passed was largely prairie, but of a rich
variety, with plenty of timber along the watercourses; it was a country
that would admit "thick & Valuable Settlements," he said. Further,
they had seen some silver ore which was supposed to be found in great
quantities on the north side of the river. The Indian leaders of several
nations were then on their way to Natchitoches.[45]

The Grand Council at Natchitoches, 1807

It is ironic that during the year of 1806 two major government exploring expeditions had been launched by the United States with orders to
seek out the Comanches and their allies, all to no effect, and then, in
the summer and fall of 1807, one band after another of those very Indians began arriving in the American city of Natchitoches. Sibley had
succeeded with his traders where Washington had failed, and his letters on the Grand Council of 1807 are understandably exultant.[46]

The first group arrived in mid-August. These were the Tawakonis
and a contingent of eighty Comanches, led by four great chiefs, none of
whom "were here before or had seen any Officer or United States
Agent." First the Comanches and then the Tawakoni leaders were invited to Sibley's home, where he smoked with them (the Comanches
would not touch liquor) and had them measured for regimental uniform
coats—scarlet ones with black velvet trim for the Comanches, buff and
blue ones for the Tawakonis. Among the many presents made them
were guns for each and medals upon which were engraved an eagle and
the seal of the United States.

The great council, preceded by the smoking of the calumet and the lighting of ceremonial fires, began on August 18. But it was prefaced by a theatrical performance which—even allowing for some exaggeration of drama on Sibley's part—still captures for us the spirit of intent of the Americans. The leading Comanche chief, before nearly three hundred Indians of varying affiliations, produced a Spanish flag, which he laid at Sibley's feet, asking to exchange it for a United States flag. When Sibley mildly protested that Spain might take exception to such an exchange, the chief replied that it made no difference to him "whether Spain was pleas'd or displeas'd" and that he would wave the American flag "through all the Hietan Nation." Sibley recounts what then transpired: "I had a flag brought which Major Freeman had left with me. I first rap'd it round Myself, gave it to him he did the Same, & embraced it with Great earnestness. . . . I at the Same time Presented him with an Elegant Belt which I had worn myselfe, took it off & put it on him which had a good Effect, as it was done in Presence of a Large Number of Indians of different Nations."[47]

The council must have been one of the high points of Sibley's career. His speech to the assembled throng was sympathetic and reassuring. The Americans were "Natives of the Same land that you are, in other words, white Indians," he told them. He was quick to point out to them that the Nacogdoches traders (Barr and Davenport) whose high prices they complained of were not Americans, and he promised them that he would soon send traders whose prices would please them. He closed by inviting the chiefs to accompany him to Washington, there to meet with Jefferson himself.

The only disappointment had been the failure of the Taovayas to attend. But that was soon ameliorated, for in October nearly one hundred of these "Panis," including Awahakei as well as a number of Comanche chiefs from nearby bands, arrived to call on him. Again Sibley played the gracious host, liberally making presents of guns, medals, and saddles, although he had only one coat and no flags left. On the twenty-fifth he had a most instructive talk with the Comanche chief Lewis had met the previous winter. Speaking Spanish, the Comanche told him that Natchitoches was too far to come to trade, but that if American traders would visit them they would be made most welcome. Horses and mules were to them "like grass," he told Sibley, and if these

were not sufficient inducement they also had buffalo robes and "knew
where there was Silver Ore plenty." And what did they ask in barter?
Guns, he said. Guns, lead, and powder to fight the Osages.

Sibley was equally candid: horses, mules, buffalo robes, and silver
ore were sure to interest American traders and would net the Indians
plenty of guns.[48]

The Glass Expedition

The stage had thus been set for what was to be the most well-provi-
sioned and ambitious trading expedition emanating from the southern
frontier since Nolan's fourth expedition in 1797–98. Although Pike's
1807 letter to the Natchez *Herald* on the imprisonment of Nolan's men
surely must have given pause to some potential traders (the Americans
could not have known of Cordero and Salcedo's new policy), nonetheless, several successful expeditions had been made, and their adventures no doubt recounted in the frontier towns. Too, there was the lure
of easy wealth. Unbroken Texas horses brought from ten dollars to several times that for exceptional animals in Natchez and Kentucky, and
who knew what sort of exotic mineral wealth might be had for the taking. Accordingly, in the spring of 1808, when Awahakei sent word to
Sibley through Dehahuit that the Taovaya-Wichitas were soon to hold a
"trading fare" at their villages, and would be pleased if American traders would attend, Sibley mentioned the invitation to Anthony Glass of
Natchez.

Something of a minor figure in early Mississippi history, Glass
must have been among the first American settlers to arrive on the
Louisiana-Mississippi frontier. Leaving relatives in Harrisburg, Pennsylvania, sometime before 1792 Glass and his brother, Andrew, had
emigrated in company with a family named Hyland to present Concordia Parish, Louisiana. Reasons and dates for this migration are not
clear; family tradition holds that the Hylands, at least, were Tories in
the American Revolution. Although they obtained a land grant in
Spanish Louisiana, by 1798 the two brothers had settled on the first
range of bluffs beyond the eastern bank of the Mississippi at the Walnut
Hills (the site of present Vicksburg).[49] They were no doubt witnesses,
perhaps admirers, of Philip Nolan's comings and goings throughout the
1790s.

In Mississippi Territory the Glass brothers became substantial citizens. Andrew was public-spirited and was chosen a delegate to the Mississippi State Constitutional Convention in 1817; from 1817 to 1827 he served as sheriff of Warren County. Anthony's interests seem to have been more pecuniary. Around 1799 he acquired and for a couple of years operated a hardware and dry-goods store in Natchez and was soon a familiar figure in that town. The documents portray a convivial, well-liked young man of means and at least some education, who was a regular customer at popular places like King's Tavern. Popular writers on Natchez have fashioned an elaborate story, based on two events occurring in 1802 and 1803, that he was "a sort of agent for outlaws" on the Natchez Trace and fenced stolen property in his store. Historical documents, although linking his name circumstantially in the affairs, hardly support such a contention, and no charges of complicity were ever brought against him.[50]

The available evidence portrays, instead, a middle-class pioneer merchant whose store in Natchez and eagerness to expand the family's land holdings at the Walnut Hills had brought him into contact with neighbors such as Robert Ashley, John House, John Davis, Jeremiah Downs, Berimon Watkins, and William C. Alexander, all of whom had already made expeditions onto the plains. In 1808 he was in his prime, around thirty-five years of age. His wife, Mary Hyland Glass, had died the year before, and a request to be allowed to settle in Spanish Texas had been denied. No doubt all of these factors help explain Glass's response to Awahakei's invitation: "Soon after [Sibley writes] Mr. Glass informed me that If he could procure at Natchitoches Suitable Goods. & I would Give him a License, he believed he would take a trip to the Panis Nation."[51]

With the exception of the two government explorations aimed at the Southwest, no other expedition in the post-Nolan age attracted the attention that the Glass foray did. There seem to have been multiple reasons for this. For one thing, Glass himself appears not to have been overly discreet about his plans, and by the summer of 1808 the rumor was widespread on the frontier that he was mounting a "silver mine expedition." Additionally, both American and Spanish officials were convinced that the expedition was much larger than it actually was. Judge John C. Carr of Natchitoches believed that Glass had assembled from 100 to 120 men and was expecting additional contingents from

Natchez and the Rapide settlement. Simon de Herrera likewise was given to understand from long-time Natchitoches informant Juan Cortes that the American party consisted of sixty men from Natchitoches, that Glass brought twenty-eight more ("well-armed") from Natchez, and that 100 more were assembling in Illinois to join them. Their objectives, according to Cortes, were to work two mines (one 300 leagues up, on the south side of the Red River, the other farther upriver and on the north bank), to which end Glass had assembled tools and equipment for "smelting silver."[52] Clearly, many individuals on both sides of the Neutral Ground considered the expedition of filibuster size; indeed, Territorial Governor Claiborne told Secretary of State James Madison that although the expedition was probably "nothing more than a plundering or Silver mine expedition set on foot by Glass . . . it may possibly be a prelude to a project of greater moment;—It has a squinting towards Burrism.—"[53]

Yet another cause for alarm, insofar as Claiborne was concerned, was the degree of government involvement in the expedition. Not only did he doubt the legality of Sibley's licensing a trade with "Spanish Indians," from Carr he had learned that Glass was calling himself "Captain" and that he had procured from officers at Fort Claiborne an epaulet, a military coat and belt, and a dress sword. It was known that he carried for delivery to the Indians an American flag, under which he planned to travel, as well as U.S. military coats and other presents, and Carr wrote that Glass insisted "that he had in his pocket a Commission from Government, and had therefore no fear of being taken by the Spaniards, or if he should, he would certainly be reclaimed by the United States whose officer he was." A circumstance Carr believed added credence to the claim was his using Sibley's note to purchase five hundred dollars worth of trade goods in Natchitoches. Such actions, Claiborne argued, were highly illegal, but his appeal to Carr to have Glass arrested before he could invade Spanish dominions came too late.[54]

Claiborne's contention that "the explanations of Doctor Sibley [respecting the Glass expedition] so far from being satisfactory, have convinced me, that he has exceeded his powers, and justify a suspicion that he is not actuated by honest views," and his repeated references to the "many unprincipled adventurers, which Burrs treasonable designs drew to the shores of the Mississippi,"[55] at length elicited a hot reply from Sibley in defense of the Glass party. Knowing better than Claiborne the wishes of the administration with respect to the interior Indians, he pointed out to Washington officials that it was "notorious" that he had been in the habit of licensing traders to the Taovaya-Wichitas. Glass had a party of only "5 or 6 other persons as hirelings or assistants, all of them Characters I knew and approved of," Sibley insisted. Further, the party "were Armed Only as hunters, or people who had to Subsist Some Months upon what game they could kill," and they planned on staying on the northeast side of the Red River all the way to the Taovaya-Wichita villages. Relative to the trustworthiness of the party, Sibley asserted that "there never has been to my knowledge so respectable a trading party taken their departure from this place, nor one on whose prudence I had such Confidence. . . . I have always calculated that good would come from it." In a final, clear reference to Claiborne, Sibley vented his frustration at the commotion: "It is vexatious that there are Amongst us persons who are never satisfied with attending to those affairs with which they have business, but busy themselves with Other affairs."[56]

That Sibley protested so strongly in defense of Glass argues, I believe, that the project was one he personally sponsored from the beginning. Almost all of the references to Glass being a "Captain"[57] come from Sibley; quite likely the difference in treatment accorded private traders as compared to Freeman and Pike had not escaped him, perhaps promoting the idea that proclaiming Glass an American officer would simultaneously engender Indian respect and protect him from potential Spanish abuse. Actually, Spanish officials saw through this strategem. What left Glass unharrassed—with one notable exception, as the journal will make clear—was the new Spanish policy of dealing with American traders only indirectly, through the Indians. Spanish officials must also have felt somewhat secure in the knowledge that at that moment a large expedition of two hundred men and eight hundred animals, led by veteran Francisco Amangual, was pushing through Texas to Santa Fe with orders to inform all the Indians encountered "that they should not trade with any other nation that may come to induce them. . . ." Likewise, Marcel Soto had been dispatched to the Taovaya-Wichitas in April to announce the new trading arrangements at Bayou Pierre.[58]

It is beyond doubt that Sibley assisted Glass in assembling men and trade goods. At least three of the party—William C. Alexander, John Davis, and the métis interpreter, Joseph Lucas—were already veterans of the Taovaya-Wichitas–Comanche trade. Glass asserts that he carried with him more than two thousand dollars worth of trade goods, indicating that possibly as much as a quarter of his Stock had been provided by the Indian agent. In a letter to Dearborn on November 20, Sibley relates that Glass "left with me a list of the Goods he took Out, all of which I found to be proper articles."[59] Unfortunately, the document seems not to have survived.

It would be highly useful to know exactly what goods and in what quantities Glass assembled to trade for Indian mustangs, and information. His journal mentions only blankets, tobacco, lead, and (on two occasions) kegs of gunpowder. Beyond that we must extrapolate Glass's circumstances in 1808 from the experiences of others. Judging from Thomas Linnard's orders from the Natchitoches trading factory during this period, Glass probably laid in a large store of blankets and brightly colored cloths, "wampum beeds," paints of different colors (vermilion was the favorite) and plenty of tobacco and tobacco boxes. Metalware, especially cookware, knives, hatchets, combs, metal mirrors, and agricultural and stockworking implements (for Caddoan herder-farmers) must have made up a considerable portion of his wares. Guns and accoutrements, however, were almost certainly his prize trade items. Liquor was illegal and was less likely to be overlooked than guns, and Sibley had found the Comanches uninterested in it in 1807.[60] Finally, Sibley gave Glass a written memorandum relative to his actions as a United States representative to the Indians. And he almost certainly encouraged him to keep the journal of his experiences, perhaps even pointing out aspects of Indian behavior and attitudes he wanted Glass to note especially.

Thus, when Anthony Glass assembled his ten men at Sibley's Salt Works, just east of Natchitoches, on the fifth of July, 1808, he was not destined to become just one more unheralded representative of the early American affair with the trans-Mississippi West. Rather, he would be able to give the United States government an idea of the nature of the southwestern country and peoples that its official explorations had been unable to provide.

The Document and Editorial Procedures

In the 1820s Professor Benjamin Silliman of Yale University began to assemble materials for an article in his *American Journal of Science and Arts* on the "Louisiana Iron," at the time the largest meteorite in any collection in the world. He wrote to Dr. John Sibley in Natchitoches, who was known to have shipped the meteorite to New York in 1810. Could Sibley provide any information on how and where the meteorite had been found? He could, Sibley wrote; in fact, he had in his possession a manuscript journal kept by the leader of the expedition of traders who were the first to be shown it by the Indians.

On June 2, 1822, Sibley forwarded to Silliman a copy, made by "a very young lady" in his household, of a twenty-eight-page manuscript journal, which Sibley had entitled, "Copy of a Journal of a Voyage from Nackitosh into the interior of Louisiana on the waters of Red River Trinity Brassos Colerado & the Sabine performed between the first of July 1808 & May 1809 By Captain Anthony Glass of the Territory of Mississippi." Whether Glass had anything to do with the titling of his journal cannot now be determined, for this quite legible copy, housed since Silliman's death in the Silliman Family Collection at Yale, is today the only extant version. Sibley seems not to have appreciated the significance of original documents, for the same fate befell the original of the Bénard de La Harpe journal, which Sibley had found and had copied in 1805.

Since the only surviving version of the Glass journal was copied under Sibley's supervision, there is justifiable cause for concern about whether he might have tampered with it. From his own admission we know that two passages—an Indian oral tradition and an appended sketch of Comanche culture—were actually authored by Sibley and added to the journal by the copyist. The Indian agent did proofread and occasionally marked the rest of the manuscript, and—unless the original in Glass's hand someday turns up—we will never know if he caused any sections of the diary to be omitted. There are some noteworthy gaps in the journal, particularly during Glass's winter hunt with the Comanches in late 1808. Perhaps there were entries here that Sibley felt might compromise them; more likely, I believe, Glass simply tired of making journal notations during this period.

Whatever else he may have been, Anthony Glass was not a literary man. Neither he nor the frontier hunters he traveled with were men likely to keep a journal of this sort. Almost certainly the idea originated with Sibley, in the Indian agent's quest to know more about the interior country and its inhabitants. Indeed, that Glass left the only copy of his journal with Sibley argues for its being a report, even if that was not the impression about it Sibley gave the government.

Lewis O. Saum writes, early in *The Fur Trader and the Indian*, that since traders often had the earliest extensive contact with Indians, and as a consequence of their calling found it necessary to learn Indian habits and preferences, their accounts ought to be used more widely. In fact, traders are now being reconsidered by ethnohistorians as possibly being a more objective source of reporting on Indian cultures than that provided by Christian missionaries, and perhaps even explorers.

Saum's litmus-test questions for trader's journals as reliable documents of ethnography are (1) how well does the trader express himself with pen, and (2) is the point of view skewed in any way because of an ulterior motive? What we are looking for is an honest and reliable account, written well enough to portray detailed word pictures. Glass was an interested and observant recorder of Indian life. Perhaps because of Sibley's influence, his point of view seems remarkably free of ethnocentric bias. If there is an ulterior motive in mind it might only be to protect Sibley, certainly not the common one of cultural put-down. He is not so subtle about which of the several Indian peoples he is disposed towards, however, so there are opinions. Glass's topographical descriptions and occasional snatches of natural history are far from scientific. But they are representative of the frontier hunter's perceptions of nature, and as such are useful and welcomed. Finally, Glass could express himself, in an earthy, sometimes halting, but often readable style. Along with its early date, these qualities make the Glass journal an important document.

In keeping with the standard practices of historical editing, the journal appears here exactly as in the manuscript version, with no changes in spelling, punctuation, or capitalization. Where no punctuation appears I have used spaces to indicate sentence breaks. Infrequently, words have been inserted to smooth meaning; these are always bracketed. Everywhere it was possible I have faithfully transcribed the words written by the copyist, choosing to ignore Sibley's occasional proofing substitutions (there were one or two interesting differences). The *only* changes I have made are to divide the journal at its two natural breaks, and to provide titles for the three parts that result.

Annotation of the journal, particularly of the sections on Indian life and the diplomacy involving them, has been undertaken with a view toward assessing the ethnohistorical and historical implications of Glass's observations. Also, because of its importance in early American environmental study, as well as for clarifying the natural history notes in the journal, Glass's route has been followed in the notes as closely as his entries make possible. Readers who wish to retrace Glass's journey can do so from my annotation using a highway map. Or for a more detailed attempt, use United States Geological Survey topographic quadrangles, scale 1:250,000, in the following order: Shreveport, Texarkana, Sherman, Wichita Falls, Abilene, Brownwood, Llano, and Dallas.

PART 2
The Journal

Natchitoches to the Taovaya-Wichita Villages, July–August, 1808

THE object of the Voyage was to trade with the Panis and Commanch Indians for which purpose a passport & Licence was obtained from John Sibley Esq of Nackitosh, United States agent for Indian affairs and the party consisted of Eleven persons;[1] Anthony Glass, George Schamp, Stephen Holmes, Ezra McCall, W. Alexander, Jacob Low John Davis, James Davis, Peter Young & Joseph White who agreed to Rendezvous & depart from the Salt Works about twenty miles from Nackitosh on the fifth day of July 1808 with sixteen Horses Packed with goods and thirty two Horses. The first day made seven miles and Camped at Caney Creek Crossing Black Lake which was found so boggy the Men had to carry the Packs.[2]

July 6th   Proceeded up Black Lake and fell into the Road leading from Nackitosh to the North, to Lake Bristino and Tulin's Vachery and camped on Cypress Bayou about 15 miles course North west. — [3]

7   This day made 10 miles over poor pine wood land one of my men killed a Deer. Camped on a Creek that falls into the Red River. — [4]

8   Made 19 miles course NW passing the Vachery of Tulin at a rich Prararie and a fine spring, passed several salt licks and Encamped at a handsome Creek. — [5]

9   Made 15 miles Course the same as yesterday. all this day passed over good high land & well watered   killed a Deer & Camped at an excellent spring. — [6]

10   Sunday made 12 & half miles NW passed a large Creek which was swimming.   a wide rich Brushy Bottom. growth Principally Hackberry, killed a very fat Deer.[7]

11   Made 8¼ Miles passing nice flats of poor White Oak Lands. met three Conchetta Indians going to the factory at Nackitosh to trade. Encamped at a beautiful Praraira.[8]

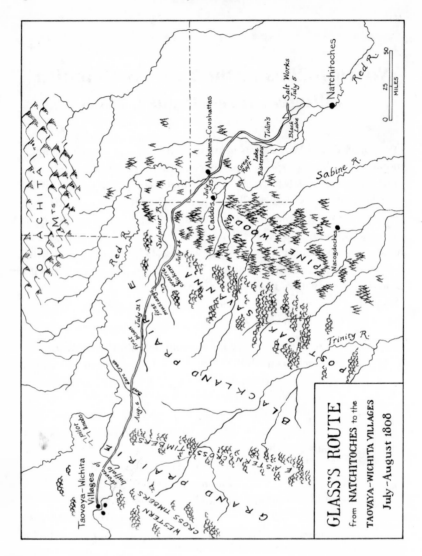

GLASS'S ROUTE from NATCHITOCHES to the TAOVAYA-WICHITA VILLAGES July-August 1808

12[h]   We lost this day one of our Men who went out to hunt [and] got Lost   we found him about three Miles from Camp. the Weather Cloudy, We killed several Deer. —

13   This day made but two Miles having to Raft a Large Bayou, Bottom wide and Boggy. —[9]

14th   Made six Miles Course WNW through the Creek Bottom   it has rained every day for eight days. —[10]

15th   Made 13½ Miles WNW passing poor Brushy Lands away along up the North East Side of Red River. Camped and found we were within one Mile of the Conchetta Village.[11]—On the East Bank of Red River, as soon as the Indians discovered us they saluted us by firing many guns and we returned the compliments. these Conchettas (as they are called) are Emigrants from the Creeks. have not long lived here. They are friendly with the Caddoes who own the Country & who used to occupy the same spot; But now live about thirty Miles South West on the Lake[12] the Caddoes left the place on account of having lost many of their People by the Small Poxe it being a custom to abandon a Village where many have died. This place is nearly in North Latitude 32, 50: and distant from Nackitosh by the usual Road about 120 miles in a rich beautiful place—

16   We entered the Village early this Morning and found about 20 men, many were out Hunting. there were a few Caddoes and Alabamos, the Chief sent for a French Interpreter, appeared Friendly: and brought a flag of the U S and hoisted it by the side of ours.[13] we crossed the River in the Evening and passed on about two miles and Encamped in a beautiful Praraira. the Country here is generally Covered with strong cane the Soil extremely rich[14]—we missed a bundle from one of our packs which we supposed an Indian had Stolen. we sent back to the Village and demanded the bundle from the Chief; they at first denied it but at length brought it out from where it was hid in the Cane near the Road. they Informed us they were fitting out a war party to go against the Ozages

Pl. XVIIII.

Cutchatés.

Alabama-Coushatta hunters, painted by Lino Sánchez y Tapia. (Courtesy Gilcrease Institute of American History and Art)

which was the cause of the firing of guns the Evening before. — [15]

July 17th   We were detained from setting off till 6 P M made about 7 miles through Rich Prarairas saw the remains of Caddo Huts and many Peach trees— [16]

18th   Our Course this day NNW through poor broken lands. — [17]

19th   Made 10 Miles NNW [and] met a Chickasaw and 4 women who informed us we were on the Road leading to the Panies from the Conchetta Village.[18] Killed a Deer.

20th   Made about 10 miles SSW along the dividing Ridge through Iron Knobby Lands. killed two Deer. we fell into the right trace and proceeded along it five miles. — [19]

21st   Made 10½ miles WNW passed a large Beaver Pond. scarcely saw a bird since we left Red River. — [20]

22nd   Course this day WNW about 9 miles. Crossed a number of Caddoes paths made by Hunting.—generally leading North and South. our trace became so dim we with difficulty could follow it. Lands Poor.[21]

23rd   Rested this day. —

24th   West 15 miles. Crossed the Road made by the Spaniards in 1807 under the command of Captain Vianne who was in pursuit of Freeman and Sparks who were ascending Red River on an exploring expedition by order of Mr. Jefferson the Hon. president of the United States. The country all allong here pretty much timbered with Ash   Oak Hickory and the soil good here and there interspersed with Rich handsome Prararies containing from 50 to 2 or 300 acres affording beautiful situations.[22]—a party of Caddoes were on the same trail about 2 days ahead of us who had so frightened away the game we killed nothing for two days since we Left the Conchetta Village. We have been on the waters of Little River now commonly called the Sulphur Fork of Red River sometimes in sight of the bottom and generally traveling up the River and parallel with it. Immense Bodies of Rich land are on this River & the three Branches of it. —

25th   This day we made 13 Miles Continuing up the Sulphur Fork of Red River and encamped in a beautiful Prararie.[23]

"The country all along here pretty much timbered . . . here and there interspersed with Rich handsome PraFor raries"—the post-oak savannah transition from
forest to blackland prairie.

26th   We made 15 miles west. Crossing the south branch of the
        Sulphur Fork in the Morning which we found about 40
        feet wide and 3 or 4 feet deep. about 5 miles from the
        River we came to a large Praraia which extends down in
        the forks of the River. anglining [?] outwards after enter-
        ing the Prarairie about three Miles. Came to a beautiful
        Lake about two Miles long, and two hundred Yards wide[24]
        we continued along the Lake & the timbered Lands to
        the right, the whole country a rich soil gently rolling.
        Killed two Deer. the flies began to be troublesome.—

27   Made 23 miles WNW finding the course of the Praraire
        too much to the south and the wood on our right very
        thick and brushy to pass through with pack horses, All
        this day we passed small mounds innumerable Elevated
        5 or 6 feet they are generally 15 or 20 feet in diameter

and rising perpindicularly. We saw this day great numbers of Prararie Hens   killed several and passed some
beautiful Lakes.—[25]

28   Course WNW 17 miles crossing the middle branch of the
Sulphur Fork of Red River. Lands very rich. we en-
camped by a Caddoe hunting path. Timber strong Oak
Hickery   Grape Vines & etc.[26]

29th   Rested this day in Camp. A wild horse came amongst
ours   three of our horses followed him off. we pursued
them five Miles and were obliged to shoot the wild horse
before ours could be recovered. one of our Men went out
to kill Buffalo and has not returned. killed two Deer.

30th   Remained in Camp this day. the lost Man returned but
had killed nothing.—

31   This day we travelled about 20 miles WNW through rich
lands and watered by a number of Beautiful Creeks some
of them we found saltish. We found this day large quantities of Excellent plumbs growing on low small trees or
rather shrubs of about 4 or 5 feet high.[27] we saw likewise
large numbers of Prararie Squirrels about half as large as
a rabbit of a greyish colour. they live under ground. rais-
ing hillocks over their houses about two feet high. Neatly
covered with sticks and grass the doors of their houses
are about 5 inches wide where a centinel is always fixed
to give notice of approaching danger, when the Males
sally out swell and bellow like a Bull but retreat as the
Enemy advance.[28]

August 1st   Made this day 20 miles WNW through a Beautiful rich
Prararie and crossed two Creeks in the bottom of which
are large quantities of the Bois d'Arck. the tree resembles an Apple tree and the fruit an Orange   the
wood is yellow like   The tree is hard takes a brilliant
polish and [is] the most Elastic of long wood known. the
Indians make their bows of it from which the french have
given it the name of Bois d'Arck or Bow Wood.[29]—here
we shot a Buffalo and two Deer.—

2nd   We rested all this day in Camp.—

A wild, native bois d'arc, "the most Elastic of long wood known." (Photograph by Kate Dowdy)

3rd   made about seven miles WNW   left two Men behind to search for a horse that we believed some Wild Horses had decoyed away.—

4   Course West North West 7 Miles   the two Men came up without the Horse. they had killed the Wild one but could not recover the one we had lost—they killed a Buffalo and brought with them some very fat meat—Passed through some beautiful Prararies and killed a Buffalo.[30]

5th   Made this day 17 miles WNW [and crossed] Boi d Arck Creek or River we supposed near 75 miles from its mouth where it falls into Red River, the Bed of the River about thirty feet wide but affords but little water except in rainy seasons. here we saw great numbers of Wild horses —and killed a Deer.[31]

6th   But 2 miles today, Course WNW   fell in with a gang of Buffalo and killed three of them, one killed by a shot

North Texas' premier bison range, the Grand Prairie.

    on Horseback at full speed. we are all well now and each Man with a Marrow Bone in his hand.—

7th   This day made about 20 miles course WNW passing about two miles through a handsome Prairies. Crossed a large Creek in each side of which is a thick wood. Stopped at twelve a clock to dine at an old Camp which two of our Men had made the fall before, and knew it to be about 50 Miles from the Panie Villages.—[32]

August
the 8th   This day we travelled Eleven Miles only, Came to Red River and crossed it at twelve o Clock the River here is about a hundred Rods wide and at this time about three feet deep. the Banks on each side very high on the North East side there are three knobbs one Elevation so high they can be seen the distance [of] thirty miles and are particularly noted by all travellers entirely overlooking all the surrounding Country. the soil rich and the Country remarkably pleasant.—[33]

9th   this day made but 3 miles. killed 2 Buffalo. Some of them seen in every direction Saw droves of Buffalo.—[34]

"Saw droves of Buffalo." This Catlin scene of wildlife in the Red River prairies was painted in the 1830s. (George Catlin, courtesy National Museum of American Art, Smithsonian Institution)

10th   WNW 18 miles. passed over Brushy lands[35] and en-
         camped about five Miles from the Panis Villages and ac-
         cording to custom dispatched a Messenger to give notice
         of our approach.—

11th   WNW five miles   the Messenger we sent to the Village
         returned early this Morning accompanied by six Indians
         and we were met by fifty men on Horseback, who Es-
         corted us into the Village[36]   when in sight of the town
         we hoisted our flag and they immediately hoisted a simi-
         lar one which they had received of Dr. Sibly of Nacki-
         tosh.[37] a man met us with an Invitation to the Chief's
         house. But we preferred encamping near the great spring
         and were conducted thither where I pitched my tent and
         hoisted my flag in front of it, about fifty yards from the
         Chiefs house.—a band of Women came immediately [and]
         pulled up and cleared away the grass and weeds from
         about the camp and also cleared a path down to the spring.

Life among the Indians,
August–October, 1808

August 11th I then waited on the Great Chief[1] and was received
with every token of Friendship   I informed him I
would wait on him again the next day & inform[ed]
him for what purpose we had come to his Country
& returned to my tent   we found our Camp
filled with a quantity of green Corn, Beans, Water
and Mus Melons.—

12 About one hundred and fifty of the head men and
women[2] were assembled at the Council House. I
repaired thither   all was silent   after a pause
through my Interpreter Lucas I spoke to them in
substance as follows:

Your Great Father the president of the United
States is still your friend and at peace with all nations and wishes you to be so likewise and will be
your father and benefactor so long as you remain
dutifull Children. The boundary line between the
United States and Spain is not yet settled; but we
expect to settle it amicably without a war; but
should we be disappointed in this expectation I advise you to have nothing to do in the dispute;[3] we
do not want your help   we are strong enough
Ourselves.— Whenever you visit us you will be
treated in the same friendly manner which you
treat us when we visit you. I have come a long Journey to see you & have brought with me some goods
to exchange with you and your brothers—the Hietans,[4] for Horses if you will trade with us on fair and
Equal terms, you will in future be supplied with
goods brought into your towns; and in token of our
Friendship and sincerity I present you with this To-

bacco to be smoked this day by yourselves and Warriors: I have nothing more to say to you at present
only that I shall be some time amongst you. I am
now and all times shall be ready to hear any thing
you may have to say. *A-wa-Ke-Kes.*—[5]

The great Chief replied in a long speech expressing
his friendship for the American People and how
much he was pleased with our Visit and to see our
National Flag waving in his land—the Great Chief
lives in the town on the North east side of the river
Called *Quich*, the situation of the town is beautiful
the land of the first quality and the water from the
abundant springs they use is excellent Issuing from
a Bluff fifty feet above the River; the Inhabitants of
this village cultivate about one hundred and fifty
acres of Land in Corn, Beans, Pumpkins, Melons[6]
& their Houses are in the form of a sugar Loaf 70 or
80 feet in diameter at the base and thirty or forty
feet high. The frames are forks and poles Lathed
and Thatched with long cypress, resembling Pipe
straw. their Beds are ranged around next to the
sides and the fire is made in the middle   the
smoke passes through a hole left in the top for that
purpose.—[7] The Chief who appears to be about 50
years of age informed me that he was born on the
Arkansas River where his nation used to live but
left that Country in Consequence of their wars
with the Osages. that they had been at war as long
as tradition Could trace.[8] he returned my visit the
same day. when he arrived a great number of Indians were round our Camp   as he approached
they all withdrew to some distance out of respect to
him. The Chief farther said that when they first
emigrated from the Arkansas they went and settled
on the river Brassos distant about five days journey where part of their nation now lived called
Tawekenoes.—[9]
The Chief of the Village [that] is situated on the op-

Left: A Taovaya chief, Sky-se-ro-ka, painted by Catlin in the 1830s. *Right*: A Taovaya woman named She-de-a, or Wild Sage. (George Catlin, courtesy National Museum of American Art, Smithsonian Institution)

A Taovaya grass-covered lodge of the type constructed by the Southern Plains Caddoans. (George Catlin, courtesy National Museum of American Art, Smithsonian Institution)

posite side of the River came over and invited me to
come over and make him a visit   I accepted the
invitation and crossed over [and] found the village
about a mile from the River and Containing Sixty
five Houses; resembling those on the other side before described—they cultivate Corn Beans Pumpkins in about 300 acres of land. the town is separated into two parts.[10] Kachatake is the name of the
Chief of one part, the Witcheta Village; and Kittsita
Commands the other division called Taweach;[11]
Chickakinik a Warrior and leader is treated by
them with the greatest respect   he has visited
lately Governor Condero of S'Antonio and held a
talk with him; and says that he told him to have
nothing to do with the Americans that they were a
designing bad people and by and by would make
war against them and would kill them all, and requested he would always inform him when any
Americans came amongst them & he would send
men and drive them away;[12] the governor likewise
told him he would let them have Soldiers to assist
them in their War against the Ozages and that they
should come the ensueing spring and that he had
already designated the place for their garrison.— I
exhibited here some goods which I told them I had
to exchange for horses   several came [and] offered horses but were not satisfied with the offers
made for them. A Chief man came up, and ordered
the Indians all away; him and the principal chief
spoke together some time and concluded that the
fault was in my Interpreter and that it was him who
made the difficulty; but they were mistaken. they
demanded more for their horses than I could afford
to give them   two men went with me to my camp
and were beginning to trade but before it was concluded the man who first made the difficulty came
and ordered them all away.—

14   The man I was endeavouring to trade with yester-

day came over this morning and took the same for his horses I had offered him the day before.—Several principal men came over and I bought about twenty horses without difficulty.—[13]

15th Bought this day thirteen Horses.

16th Sent out our Horses about twenty miles to pasture.

17th Visited the Villages on the South side of the River and was treated plentifully with Excellent Melons the best they had to offer.—

18 All in Camp   no occurrence.

19 Sent more horses out to the drove.

20th Spent all this day in Camp; Melons plenty.

21st The Queens with a number of women made us a visit   they brought with them a parcel of poles and made with them an Elevated place [for us] to sleep on such as they use themselves.—

22nd Continued trading for horses and sending them to the Cavirllard.

23rd The Men who were out guarding the Horses came in this morning and reported that a party of Osages had stolen twenty nine of them, and the best we had   one of them was tied with a Cabras (Halter) close to their Camp—the Men followed them five or six miles but could not come up with them. they believed from the trail that there were a Dozen of them.—

24 & 25 nothing occured.

26th We heard of a small party of Hietans some distance off and some of our party sett off to buy horses from them.

27 & 28 & 29 Remained in Camp and nothing occured.

30th The same Men returned from the Hietans with Eleven good Horses they had bought.—

Sept th 1st We moved our Cavirllard over to the south west side of the river. a party of the Hietans arrived to buy corn of the Pawnees. they made several Horse and foot races. [The Hietans] are great Jockies but when beaten freely give up the stakes.

2^d & 3^d All well in Camp.

4th Six of our Party with a Chief & the king's son satt off for the Lower Hietans with five packs of goods to purchase Horses and three men started with our Drove of Horses toward the Trinity River about thirty miles distant. Myself McCall and Lucas the Interpreter remained in Camp.—[14]

5th Moved up to the Chief's house and am now more Comfortable. the Chief is in our Mess   we want nothing the town affords. Pitched my tent on a scaffold made for the purpose.—

6th Met the Chiefs of the west side of the River in Council. some of the Company was displeased at the offer I had made him for his horse and said he would go and Inform the Spaniards that we were here—a Woman replied you may go and inform them but if they come here to interrupt our trading with these Americans I myself will kill their Captain   the other then said if that is your talk I don't go. Pawnees pen their horses every night. each family have a pen close to their houses. Not withstanding all their precautions the Osages frequently steal away their Horses in the night. their Warfare appears to have no other object but Stealing and plunder   they don't kill if they can attain their Object without it. About a month ago they [the Osages] came and hoisted two flags between the Villages in the Day about 12 o Clock one Red and the other White and drove off about five hundred horses. they appeared so strong that the Pawnees did not think proper to sally out and attack them.—[15]

7th At Camp all this day   nothing occured.

8th This Morning about Day brake the time the Pawnees generally let their Horses out of the pens a party of Ozages who were watching drove off thirteen Horses; after a great Parade in getting ready a party turned out and followed them. Being desirous to see the pursuit and what kind of soldiers they are I got my Horse and followed them—We followed their trail five Hours and a half generally in full gallop but saw none of them. found where they had killed a Buffalo and cut off some of the meat we judged from the appearance of the fire [that] they had left that place about three quarters of an hour   we returned to the village about 12 o Clock very much fatigued   they [the Panies] appeared to have no regular mode of turning out. as one got ready he sat out. their manner of making Signals is worthy of note, which is by wheeling their Horses in a variety of manners and directions on a Hill so that those in the rear can Discover at the Distance of five, Eight, or ten miles and those who are appointed to give the signals are placed so that they can see each other and by this they will communicate the number and strength of the Enemy, of what Nation they are, whether Encamped or moving, and if moving in what Direction [16]   not more than thirty of the Party that went out had guns   the rest had Bows and Arrows. They are likewise at war with the Tawenatas. [17] the Panies have amongst them a number of Prisoners from those nations and some others most of whom they Compell to labour like slaves.—

9th   This day I was engaged in witnessing the mode these Indians have to Physic themselves—when they think they require it they drink a large quantity of Warm Water and Repeat it for several mornings successively Vomiting it up immediately after they have drank it [18]—There are amongst the Panies an uncommon number of Blind Persons accasioned as they suppose from the air in Dry weather being filled with a fine dust raised by the wind from the Extensive sand Beaches which in low water are exposed—Men who want wives generally purchase them of the Uncle or Brother of the woman. the

An Osage warrior. Catlin called him Tal-lee. (George Catlin, courtesy National Museum of American Art, Smithsonian Institution)

general price is one or two Horses. But if a stranger buys a Wife he must pay for her in Straw, Blankets, Vermillion & Beads.[19] the husband always dresses the Wife as he pleases. But they are great Libertines both men and Women, not addicted to Jealousy and nothing is more common than for a Man to loan or hire out his Wife; particularly to Strangers who visit the nation.[20] They differ from almost all other Savages in another particular; the Men labour in the Field with the women and make all the fences, which are made by driving stakes in the Ground three or four feet apart and wattling brush into them.— They have no cattle nor hogs and only Horses and Mules to fence against,[21] they raise much more corn Pumpkins and Beans than for their own use   they always have [a surplus] to exchange with the Hietans for Horses and Mules. the Pumpkins are pressed by cutting them round in large strings and when wilted is woven or plaited into a kind of Cloth, and they carry it with them when they travel, or go out a Hunting[22] they make very little use of any other Animal food than Buffalo meat. Deer not being hunted are very plenty about their Villages and tame like Domestic animals— The men have as many wives as they please and put them away when they please and the women have the same Liberty with their husbands. The head warriors can take any women they please   Men of 50 and sixty are often seen with wives not more than fifteen; men and their wives never sleep together in less than 7 or 10 moons after the Birth of a child, this they say is to prevent the Children from being sickly. the Husband in the mean time keeps two or three women in the same house. There are in this nation many more women than men. during our stay in the town there were several deaths. When one Died a Natural Death they bury all their small trinkets with them and Instead of filling up the graves a bank with forks and poles is raised over them and none but the relatives of the deceased are allowed to mourn over them; But when one is killed by an enemy all the nation cry   they mourn three days and then smoke and all is over[23]—when one kills an enemy he

brings home with him pieces of his flesh and whoever he gives it to become United with him as long
as they live.[24]— English goods are brought to this
nation by a tribe of trading Indians who live on the
waters of the ~~Mississippi~~ Missoury called *Owaheys*
who bring their goods from English traders from
the Lakes of Canada.[25]— During our stay at the
Panies Villages we lived in plenty. fresh Buffalo
meat was brought in every day—they dry their
Corn on a scaffold erected for the purpose and each
house has put up from an hundred to an hundred
and fifty bushels. and when it is sufficiently dry
they pick it up in bags made of the skins of Buffalo
& if they leave the Village in winter as they generally do they bury these bags of Corn in the ground
and so artfully cover up the place that if an Enemy
should in their absence come and lay waste their
towns they would not find their Corn.—[26] Their
forts are of a very slender construction made of
mud, which they retire to when attacked by an enemy.[27] they have about 3 hundred warriors. and in
the Village nearly two thousand Souls with a large
proportion of children, and some very old persons[28] They are not addicted to stealing but if any
small theft is committed and they are caught or
detected they give up the article stolen with a
smile.—

They have a story of the Orphan[29] which they often
repeat, in order to preserve a kind of traditional
record from generation to generation, they say some
ages ago when they lived on the river Platt, that
falls into the Missouri they had been so harrassed
by their wars with the Ozages and some other tribes
that they resolved to move to the south so far that
their enemies could not find them, [They] accordingly prepared and satt off, there was a little Orphan Boy whose parents and relations had all been

killed by their Enemies, as they were leaving their
Village forever, no provision had been thought of to
take the little boy along   every one seemed already
to have too many encumbrances,—an old Man who
had no family offered to take him, and they sett off
on foot for at that time they had no horses, in all
possible haste as though they were flying from the
Enemy and proceeded through the tall grass the
Pararies resembling the Ocean, every one getting
along as he Could, the little boy was too small to
walk, and the Old Man had to carry him.— they
made a halt after a long March and collected some
Buffalo dung to make the only fuel these immense
[prairies] afford—and after resting a short time and
fearful of being overtaken by an enemy sett off
again. the old man being extremely fatigued &
nearly exhausted delayed setting off with the main
band, thinking he would rest a few minutes longer
and remained by the fire till the company were out
of sight and to amuse his little comrad began to sing
a song and soon [the orphan boy] fell asleep. the
poor old man finding himself all alone and separated from his people expecting the Enemy might
be on the trace any moment to appear in sight was
in the utmost perplexity of mind. Exhausted as he
was, to carry the boy and overtake the company
was impossible. to remain with him, both would be
lost, he looked upon the sleeping Orphan and wept
at the resolution he was about forming to go and
leave him. he kissed him and wept over him. turned
his back advanced in the Path a few steps. turned
Back resolved and resolved at length [and] after one
great effort sat off. the Company after some time
missing the old man and his Charge made a halt—.
the old man came up, a thousand tongues Instun-
taneously demanded what have you done with the
little Orphan Boy? the Old Man almost breathless
interrupted by sighs and tears told them, "that he

had left him asleep by the fire where they had stopped.["] every young man volunteered their services to go back and bring him, all the women and his little comrads calling Out to those setting off to make haste—they soon found the fire and saw the print where the boy had slept, believing he had awakened and strayed off in the tall grass they divided to search for him in every direction. in vain they sought and were about giving it out under the belief that some wild beast had taken him off bodily when they heard him singing the song he was singing with the old man when he fell asleep Their hearts were instantly gladdened thinking they would have him and be on their return, but on pursuing the voice they could not find him, after hunting for some time [they] became frightened and were about tracing their way back to the Company waiting. when they heard the Voice of the Boy, directing them to go to an Eminence in sight and look beyond it, they did so and saw (as they supposed) an imme[n]se Valley covered with ice being more and more alarmed it being in summer [and] the weather warm they regarded the ice as a miracle; being about to leave it they heard the voice of the Boy again tell them what they saw was not ice but something the great spirit had placed there for the good of mankind, they tasted and found it salt. the voice spoke again and told them to carry some of it to their Company and search no more for him for he was no longer mortal, and was with the great spirit. The party returned to their company in waiting and related [?] the story, some of them took a Journey every year to the grand saline which they call the miracle and every night to this day they sing the song of the Orphan.—

Sept. 10 · 11 ·   Continued in town nothing worth remarking oc-
12 · 13th   curred.—

14th   The river has risen considerably and continues rising—Two Nandaco Indians arrived from Nacacdo-

ches [30]—the Chief myself and some others crossed
the river over to the Witcheta village where we
were to see them. I put my cloathes on a Deer skin
swam and dragged the bundle after me.— the river
is here 5 hundred yards wide and the current rapid
and at this time 12 feet deep and from the rapidity
of the current and often shifting its channel from
one side to the other the navigation is and must
ever be difficult. the Indians this day killed 41 Buffalo: the whole of the gang that made their appearance in sight of the towns; when they discovered
them fifty men on Horseback sallied out and killed
the whole without firing a gun. they always hunt
Buffalo on Horseback with spears or Bows and Arrows, they are dexterous Horsemen and have Excellent Horses. Each man singles out his victim and

"[They] killed the whole without firing a gun." (George Catlin, courtesy National Museum of American Art, Smithsonian Institution)

in full speed rides alongside of him either kills him with the spear which he carrys in his hand the handle 8 or 10 feet long or drives an arrow through him—I have seen an Indian with a Bow of the Boi' d Ark wood, the most Elastic wood in the world, drive an arrow entirely through a Buffalo with more force than a riffle would have sent a Ball.—[31] The Panies are singular in their mode of putting their prisoners to Death—they have a post planted in the ground about two hundred yards from the village, they strip the prisoner naked and tie him to the post. they some time remain [there] and all the people come to see him, after the women and children with sticks fall to beating him and beat him till he expires under their blows. They then cut the flesh from the Bones and hang it up in pieces in 2 different parts of the village—they never kill a prisoner who has not arrived to years of maturity young ones are made slaves or adopted into families as is generally practiced by savages.—[32]

On the Winter Hunt,
October, 1808–March, 1809

[Sept.] 15th, 16   remained in camp and nothing occured except be-
17 & 18th   ing informed by several of the Indians of a remarkable piece of metal some days journey distant to the
southward on the waters of River Brassos.—[1]

19   Hearing more of this singular metal to which they
attributed singular virtues in curing diseases I resolved to obtain permission to see it if I could and
proposed to them to go with me. this they would
not listen to. there is amongst them a Spaniard of
the name of Tatesuck who was taken prisoner when
a child and raised amongst them, he was some years
ago Liberated and might have gone where he
pleased, but knowing no other language than theirs
he concluded to remain with them, he became the
most distinguished man in the nation as a warrior
and the first Leader of war parties and is really a
Brave, Subtle and intrepid man and his Wife a
Panie woman [is] as remarkable for her address and
intrigue.—[2] This Couple became my most intimate
acquaintance   I made them some presents and obtained from them a promise to shew me this extraordinary piece of metal, for the more I heard
about it the more my anxiety was increased sus-
pecting from their account of it and great veneration for it, it might be Platina or something of great
value, no white man at this time had seen it; This
day the Party of our People who went to trade with
the Hietans returned and suspected that the Indian
guide they had with them had refused to guide
them to the Hietan Camp.—
This day to the 27th we were stationary at the Village   nothing extraordinary happening.—

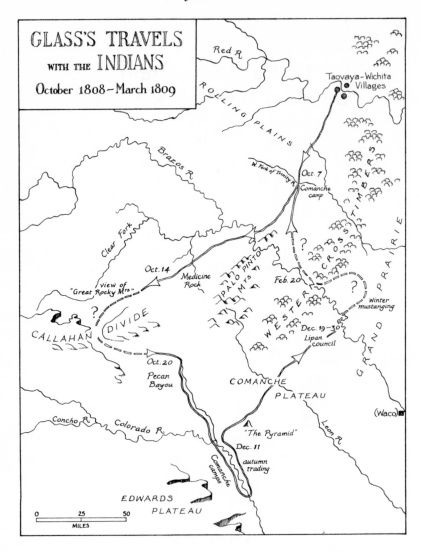

GLASS'S TRAVELS
WITH THE INDIANS
October 1808–March 1809

Red R.

ROLLING PLAINS

Taovaya-Wichita
Villages

CROSS TIMBERS

Brazos R.

W. Fork of Trinity R.

Oct. 7

Comanche
camp

Clear Fork

Oct. 14

Medicine
Rock

PALO PINTO MTS

?

Feb. 20

view of
"Great Rocky Mts"

?

DIVIDE

CALLAHAN

WESTERN

GRAND PRAIRIE

Winter
mustanging

Dec. 19-30
Lipan
council

Oct. 20

Pecan
Bayou

COMANCHE

PLATEAU

(Waco)

Concho R.   Colorado R.

Leon R.

"The Pyramid"

Dec. 11

autumn
trading

Comanche camps

EDWARDS
PLATEAU

0   25   50
MILES

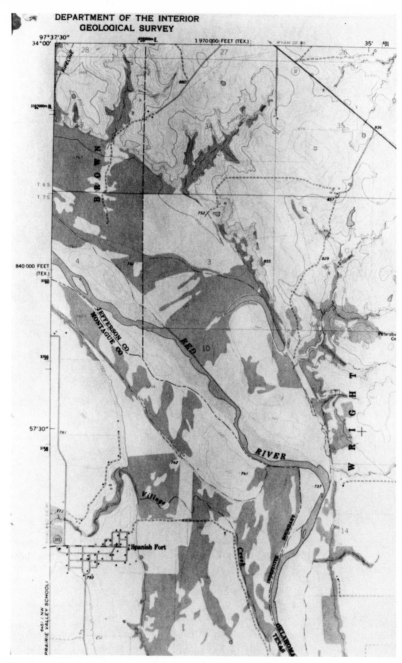

Modern U.S. Geological Survey topographic map showing the location of the historic Taovaya and Wichita villages on the Red River.

"His-oo-san-ches" (Jésus Sánchez?), a Comanche. Like Tatesuck, one of many captive Spanish children who grew up among the Plains Indians. (George Catlin, courtesy National Museum of American Art, Smithsonian Institution)

Sept 28th   A Party of Ozages made their appearance on Horse-
             back advancing directly to the village as though it
             was their intention to enter it, but it was soon dis-
             covered that their only object was to get between
             the Village and some of the Panie Horses so as to

cut them off, which they effected and drove of[f] a
number. the Panis sallied out upon them and killed
one of them and [the] Ozages wounded a Pani so
that he died the next day. Amongst the Horses was
a very valuable one of mine   We were persuaded it
was the same Party who stole our Horses on the
22nd of August   one of them was riding a remarkable Paint Horse that used to be my own riding
Horse, which was stolen with those on the 22^d of
August—The Ozage Indian that was killed was cut
in pieces and distributed through the different Villages and all the men women and children danced
for three days.

Sept 29th 30th   Oct 1st   In camp preparing to move.—

Oct 3^d   Satt off for an Hietan Camp and had proceeded but
a small distance and encamped for the night south
westerly from the Witchetta Village   when the
Panis found we were removing our goods a number
came up to see us and began begging for something,
the Wicheta Chief demanded a keg [of] Powder and
said that if we refused to comply [he] said we should
not travel on his side of the River. But he compro-
mised for a small quantity.—

4th   Rose early to pursue our Journey, in packing a Horse
broke loose amongst the others threw his Pack and
so frightened the other Horses that were packed,
that another threw his Pack and burst a keg of Powder and all was Lost.—we travelled this day about
10 miles and encamped at a stoney creek in a handsome Prarie.—[3]

5th   Travelled about 12 miles course SW   passed several fine streams of running water and encamped at
a small creek—[4] the Lands but indifferent.—

6th   Made eight Miles and encamped on a Creek, course
the same   the Lands better than yesterday—Tim-
ber scarce.[5]

7th   Made 12 Miles on a creek where Awahakea the
Panie Chief had collected a party of Hietans to

"Their tents are round like a wheatstack." A Comanche village. (George Catlin, courtesy National Museum of American Art, Smithsonian Institution)

trade with us[6]   we found about twenty tents they are made of different sizes of Buffalo Skins and supported with Poles made of red Cedar, light and neat which they carry with them. their tents are round like a wheatstack and [they] carry their tents always with them. I presented the Hietan Chief with some Blankets and trinkets—he received them apparently with an ill grace, he is a very large man and ill looking—the Hietans proceeded on with us the subject of the mass of metal was spoken of by the Hietans. They made some objections to showing it—they agreed that the Panies who found it had the best right to it but that the land where it is belongs to the Hietans   some altercation took place about it but it was finally agreed that if [it] should turn out to be of considerable value what it brought should be divided between them. several times the Indian who claimed the right of being the finder of

"He is a very large man and ill looking." George Catlin painted this Comanche chief, Ta-wah-que-nah, in 1834. (Courtesy National Museum of American Art, Smithsonian Institution)

it and who had agreed it should be showed to us Refused to proceed and I was obliged to flatter and bribe him to go on—Our whole party now became very numerous containing of men women and children near one thousand souls and three times that number of Horses & Mules, most of them were tied

A Comanche camp on the move. (George Catlin, courtesy National Museum of American Art, Smithsonian Institution)

with Ropes made of Buffalo skins every night.—It was impossible to remain at the same place but a short time on account of the Grass being soon Eaten up.

9th–14th Moving slowly on to the west through a hilly broken country which is fit only for pasturage. crossing the river Brassos about fifty miles we approached the place where the metal was; the Indians observing considerable ceremony as they approached we found it resting on its heaviest end and leaning towards one side and under it were some Pipes and Trinkets which had been placed there by some Indians who had been healed by visiting it.[7] the mass was but very little bedded in the place where we found it—. there is no reason to think it had ever been moved by man, it had the colour of Iron, but no rust upon it. The Indians had contrived with Chisels they had made of old files to cut off some small pieces which they had hammered out to their fancy. there has been no other found near it nor any thing resembling it. the surrounding country is barren Hilly, no timber but dwarf musquette, filled with grey and reddish granite Rock.[8] not having the means of ascertaining its precise quality, only, that it was obedient to the magnet—. very malable would take a brilliant polish and give fire with a flint. I had some small scales cut off and left it. The Indians informed me they knew of two other smaller pieces of the same kind of metal one about thirty miles distant and the other fifty.—[9] about twenty miles west of it there is a great appearance of Iron Ore and the country exhibits strata of shells which were pronounced to be Cokle shells by all of our party.[10]—The Country entirely Prarie. we have not seen a spring since we left the Pani Towns Many of the streams do not run but there is an abundance of standing water   not being able to purchase Horses of those Hietans our Party became discontented

"Red River," once a healing shrine of the Indians, was the largest meteorite in any collection in the world for most of the nineteenth century. It is a rough cone 40″ × 16″ × 24″. (Courtesy Peabody Museum of Natural History, Yale University)

and they all except Peter Young and Joseph Lucas
the Interpreter Left me asking some of the goods
and went in search of a larger horde of Hietans of
whom they expected to Purchase what Horses and
Mules they wanted[11]

1808 October 14　Journal continues

Here I found myself at the distance of many hundred miles from any white settlement surrounded
by thousands of Indians with nearly two thousand
dollars worth of merchandise and a large drove of
Horses and Mules fatting away in flesh and no assistance but Young and Lucas　but all the Indians appear very friendly and say they will not leave me as
long as they can be of service to me. and some say
they will go with me to Nackitosh and not only assist
me in driving my Horses but assist me also in Pur-
chasing more.—[12] we expect to meet in a short time
a large Band of Hietans. We continue to travel
southwesterly and always in sight of the great Rocky
mountains.[13] the soil not very rich but the grass excellent.—This morning discovered a smoke and
awakened the Panie Chief and Lucas supposing it to
be an Hietan camp set off to ascertain it and our
whole Band sett off in the same direction though
moving slowly.—

20 and 21st　Arrived at a large Creek a branch of Colerado where
my friend the Panie chief and Lucas appeared and
reported that they had seen a large band of Hietans
moving and that we would soon fall in with them.—
Here we gathered as many Pacans as we pleased
the ground was covered with them, being no other
timber on the creek bottom than Pacan—Here we
rested two days.—[14]

22nd　The Panie Chief and Lucas sett off again; and there
came to our camp some of the Hietans; on the 24th
they returned with a party of them and said the
whole Band would join us in a few days and continue with us till we had exchanged all our goods for
Horses and mules.—

Seen across the roll of the plains, the Callahan Divide appeared to Glass to be the "great Rocky mountains."

28ᵗʰ A large party of Hietans came to us. they amused themselves at night by a kind of gambling at which a great number of Horses and Mules were lost and won. the game was very simple and called hiding the Bullitt, and the adverse party guesses which hand it was in: they are very dexterous at this kind of gaming [15]—we continued together—The number of Hietans have been increasing at our camp for some days: we have with us now ten Chiefs and near six hundred men with a large proportion of women and children. I meet with them every day and we hold long conversations together—they profess great friendship for the Americans or Anglos as they call us. [16] Some of those who are now with us were of the Party who visited Nackitosh last year and are highly pleased with the treatment they

A Comanche chief. This was Ee-shah-ko-nee, headman of one of the Oklahoma bands. (George Catlin, courtesy National Museum of American Art, Smithsonian Institution)

received from Doctor Sibley the Indian agent and say they intend to repeat their visit. they are very desirous of trading with us but say Nackitosh is too far off.—[17]

December 7th   This day arrived an Hietan from St. Antonio and said he understood that the Spaniards and Americans were going to war and that there had been a battle near Nacadoches.[18] the Indians affect great indifference at hearing it and discover no disposition to have anything to do with our disputes. though they express warmly their good wishes for the Anglos (as they call us). and the same evening arrived several Panies who say they have lost one of the principal men a head warrior on hearing this the Panies set up a cry which they continued for three Hours and the friends or relations of the Deceased gave to those who cried with them their Blankets and flaps. these Indians are on their way to the Lepans who live not far from St. Antonio.[19] the weather has been cold and rainy and trade dull the Indians are unwilling to part with their best Horses.—

11th This morning changed our course North East towards the Panie Villages keeping altogether. Made about six miles. continuing on our march until the 19th.—[20]

19th Last night an Hietan Indian stole from us five Blankets we applied to the Chief to try to recover them but the Chiefs had ran away with them in the night—The Indians gamble every night the Panies are generally the winners. The Chief of the Lower Hietans who visited Nackitosh last fall has this day Joined us and says that the spaniards have treated him very civil since he made that visit he is a great friend of the Americans.—

Dec 19th the Indians have taken my drove of Horses entirely under their care untill I sett off for home—two Indians who live near St. Antonio (Lepans) arrived in our Camp and called the chiefs together in Council I was present, one of the strangers then informed them that they were sent by the governor of St. Antonio to cut off my head and carry it to him. After a minute or two Tatsuck my friend the great Panie warrior arose and addressed himself to the one who last spoke as follows—You want a Head do

A Lipan Apache, painted by Texas artist Friedrich Richard Petri. (Courtesy the
Texas Memorial Museum, Austin)

American hunters tend their horses in a plains village in this Alfred Jacob Miller painting, "Picketing Horses." (Courtesy Walters Art Gallery, Baltimore)

you? to carry to the Spanish governor? if you do I advise you to get your own cutt off and have it sent to him: I farther tell you that this american is my friend and if you offer the least harm to him I will soon cut your head off—There was not another word said on the subject and the governors messengers disappeared in a few minutes.[21]—a Hietan from some of the upper hordes[22] arrived and says that some of his nation have lately been to St. Antonio and stolen a large number of Horses and Mules and says that the Spaniards and his own people are on bad terms and that at the coming of new grass something will be done: they understand likewise that the spaniards and United States are going to war. I advised them in case it should happen to have Nothing to do in the quarrel.—

An Hietan this morning caught his wife in bed with a man of his party. he immediately shott him dead and then deliberately loaded his gun and shott his Wife also. some of the relations of those killed cried for a short time and all was over. this would not have happened among the Panies. they are more generous to one another. the Hietans often kill their wives so that in their camps they are more men than women—but with the Panies the contrary.—[23]

Dec. 30th The Hietans this day stole twenty three head of my Horses and say they lost that number when at Nackitosh.[24] the Panies are not addicted to stealing and have done all in their power to prevent the Hietans. they run them off in the night.—We have now left the waters of the Colerado and are now on the Brassos a broken hilly country no wood but Musquette except in the river or creek bottoms—the country is excellent Pasturage but good for little else—about ten miles from the river Brassos [Colorado] on the east side about one hundred miles from the Panie Villages in about a south west direction, in an extensive Knobby Prarie, there is a mound of a Pyramid form about four hundred feet in diameter at the base and rising to the height of about three hundred feet, caped on the top with a limestone Rock of about thirty feet in diameter in the upper side of which there is a Cavity or Bason that will contain three or four hoggsheads of water in which clear cool water is always found   when I mentioned to the Indians that it was rain water they were displeased and said no, the Great Spirit always kept it full of water for the Benefit of Travelling Indians. this Pyramid is formed by nature and the whole body seemed entirely composed of Granite Rock, the sides of it entirely Barren   not a blade of grass or shrub upon it and the cap in which is the Reservoir of water occupied the whole top of

Glass's description of the Colorado River fixes him in the Hill Country phase of its drainage.

Modern Boys Peak, probably the central Texas "Pyramid" Glass ascended in December, 1808. Juniper increase on the peak is a result of the end of the natural fire ecology.

the Pyramid   I ascended to it and drank of the
water in the Bason, though not without much difficulty and fatigue. The Prospect from it I found most
beautiful entirely overlooking the whole Country
round it for thirty or forty miles, indeed nothing
but the arck of the Horizon appears to bound the
prospect.[25] the Country appears rich in Pasturage
and well watered, with Copses of wood on the
water courses—about twenty five miles from the
Pyramid [on the] south west side of the river Brassos there is a salt spring where a considerable quantity of coarse salt may at any time be found on the
surface of the ground over which the water flows.
salt springs or licks are found near this River the
water of which is too salt to be drank.—

The river Colerado we found about fifty miles from
the Brassos, the country between these two rivers
is generally hilly Limestone in abundance, mostly
Prarie a small proportion of rich soil and all most
excellent Pasturage—[26] we traveled along in the
Colerado bottom about sixty miles   found it rich
and beautiful the timber generally Pacan and Grape
Vines. [A] Waggon load of the Pacan nut might be
gathered. the ground was covered with them: the
banks do not appear to overflow   the bed of the
River about 50 yards wide, the water clear and excellent to drink: I never saw in any country more
beautiful [situations for] settlements than might be
made on this River. I suppose we were about four
hundred miles from its mouth and it is too full of
Rocks Rapids and Shoals where we are to admit of
any kind of navigation—the Colerado

Dec 30   and Brassos head no very great distance apart. and
all in the high Lands that divide their waters from
those of the river Grand[27]—The River Trinity heads
within three or four leagues of the Panie Villages in
the Prarie the water limestone and remarkable for
its transparency and sweetness; there is a western

Branch of the Trinity that heads about thirty miles from the Panies villages in a hilly country alternately prairie and Scrubby Oak range [illegible] Lands.[28] on the river and Creek bottom most excellent settlements might be made: embracing all the advantages that could be desired in respect to soil, water, Climate and health but too great a distance from Navigation—The River Sabine heads in rich Praries about sixty miles south east of the Panie Villages   it is made by the union of several branches on which no country affords a more delightful tract of Country.—[29]

I received some of my Horses that the Indians had stolen by means of the Exertions of the Chiefs and I believe they did all in their power to prevent their people from stealing—The weather is extremely cold   stagnant waters are frozen an inch thick. we are nearly in north Lattitude 31.—The country considerably elevated and open and the cold severely felt[30]—here we attempted to pen some wild Horses which are seen by the thousands and finished a strong Pen for the purpose but the Buffalo were so plenty and so in the way we succeeded badly in several attempts[31]—The Hietan that Lucas took some stolen Horses from Came last night in our Drove and stole four—The Hietans keep with us still and we move slowly   the weather extremely cold—The Buffalo have very much eaten out the grass, my horses are falling away, the snow is now six inches deep[32]—we attempted again to catch wild Horses and failed, we were in that pursuit several days, but four more Horses stolen.—

Feb 6th   The Hietans and Panies have parted. some of the former stole from me more of my Horses. I followed them to their Camp. the Chiefs did all they could to recover them for me. but the thieves run off with them. The principal Chief told me he was truly sorry but that there were bad men in all nations, and amongst them they have no laws to punish stealing and begged I would not condemn a whole nation for the bad conduct of a few individuals, that when he was in Nackitosh he had a number of Horses stolen. but he did not think the less of us as a nation and hoped I would have the same consideration towards them.—

Feb 8ᵗʰ The Hietan Chief sent a man back with some of my Horses that had been stolen. I gave the man a Blanket some powder and lead. Tatesuck the Panie warrior having lost some Horses concluded to make a halt while the rest of the party proceeded on and I remained with him fer the same purpose. our camp reduced to six persons—Young, Lucas myself and three Panies.—

12ᵗʰ A party of Hietans came to our camp who have come directly from St. Antonio and [illegible word] say the spaniards have poisoned five of their men who are dead and [they] appear much dissatisfied and are glad the Americans have found them out: they say the spaniards told them to tell all the Panies and Hietans who have been with me never to shew themselves at St. Antonio and the same message has been sent to all the different bands of Indians in the quarter.—here we attempted again to pen wild Horses and failed.

15ᵗʰ Young, Lucas and myself left the Indians and moved on towards the Panie Villages—on the 20ᵗʰ we arrived at the Brassos where we concluded to rest for a short time: the Pasturage being better. The water salt which we thought would be a benefit to our Horses—The Indians have rejoined us and we travel on together;[33] apprehending some danger from the Tanveratas a nation at war with the Panies.[34] arrived at the Panie Villages. Four days before our arrival a party of Ozages had been there [and] attacked the Village, killed two men and took away a number of Horses　amongst them were three of mine I had left there. The St. Antonio or Lower Hietans stole from me in all forty one horses.—[35] we remained here untill the 21st of March when we sett off for Nackitosh our Horses being so very poor we were obliged to travel very slowly.—

Character of the Hietan Indians[36]

These Indians especially differ from any others in this part of America—They are rather Barbarians than savages living entirely on the flesh of Buffalo. they plant nothing. have no fixed residence. [They] are divided into many bands or Hords, extending from the waters of Red River westwardly to Calafornia on the Pacific. they have very little knowledge of themselves or even the number of Bands, each band containing from one to four thousand souls and twice [?] that number of Horses & Mules.[37] Most of their animals they tie every night with ropes made of Buffalo skins to stakes drove down in the grass round about their camp, thus they never can remain but a short time in the same place; but must move to fresh pasturage.[38] Each family have a tent made of Buffalo skins dressed white they pitch them in regular order and their camps have a handsome appearance and when the order is given to move no regular army strike their tents with more Dexterity and regularity; one Horse and mules is allotted to carry the tent, Poles, hooks, & c.—Some of the men of this nation are remarkably large and very fat—Many of them both men and women are nearly as fair as Europeans with long straight sandy or light Hair with blue eyes and freckles. I have seen many women so fair that if they were taken into the United States and dressed like American women and kept a short time out of the sun no one would ever suspect they had a drop of Indian blood in them. Yet the Chief asserts they are pure Hietans. they are many shades whiter than their Neighbours the Spaniards.—[39] The condition of women is much worse than in any other tribe I ever saw. they are kept constantly and Laborously employed in attending their Horses Mares and Colts [and] gathering their fuel, Cooking, dressing Buffalo and Antalope skins making and mending their tents & Saddles they dress the skins of the Antelope most beautifully and Colour them of every shade from light Pink to Black of which they make their own and

Husbands Clothing, some of which they cut out very ingeniously in
open work[,] the edges Pinked and scalloped resembling lace   I have
often seen them Black in so neatly Blacked and so neatly dressed unless you were to feel and examine them particularly you would take
them for fine Black Velvet   I offered a woman once twenty dollars for a
short petticoat and she laughed at me.[40] When a woman is married her
hair is cut off close to her head and platted in with the Hair of her husband. I saw a chief who had twelve wives and wore the Hair of every
one of them, in that manner, in an hundred handsome Platts reaching
down to his feet, and covering him entirely as with a mantle or Cloak
I gave him a hat and the largest I could find, but he could not get it on
his head and was obliged like a beau of the last century to wear it in his
hand. Their Language is Gutterall and Barren and they will converse
together for hours entirely by signs without a single sound.

PART 3
Epilogue

The Saga of the "Texas Iron"

A metal has been discovered about 100 miles distant from the
Pawnee villages that are on red river . . . [by] A Mr. Glass who
. . . observes that it may be procured in large quantities & that
the Indians make use of it to point the arrows. . . . I rather think
this is what was said to be the silver ore that abounds in the tract
of country occupied by the Panies. . . .[1]

Another diety was an iron man that was found by the Skiri
[Skidi] somewhere in the south. . . . and [near it] there were
many presents spread upon the ground. When the Skiri found it
and gave native tobacco to it they were successful in their raids
against the enemy. So they added this to their list of gods. Later
the image disappeared and the ceremonies were discontinued.[2]

DRIVING his herd of semiwild Indian ponies and mustangs, Glass and
his fellow traders, the métis Joseph Lucas and (now) sixteen-year-old
Peter Young, made the trip back to Natchitoches by the first week of
May, 1809. Their return, it is certain, produced considerable excitement not only among other hunter-traders but also among the officials
in that frontier post. Partly this was because both groups were impressed by Glass's success among remote plains tribes supposedly
under Spanish control. Beyond that, Glass's return with specimens of a
heavy, silvery metal that no one could identify positively, gave his journey a widespread notoriety rivaling that of some of Philip Nolan's expeditions of a decade earlier.

Dr. Sibley wasted no time lodging an official report of the expedition, and the find, with William Eustis, secretary of war in the new
Madison administration. On May tenth he composed a letter to the
government that concluded:

Capt Glass has just returned here from a Trading Voyage Amongst the Panis
& Hietan Nations of Indians, who Inhabit the Country towards the head of Red
River, and reports that the Panis & Hietans appear particularly Attached to the
Government & People of the United States, during his Travels & residence
amongst the Indians where he spent more than Eight Months he was Con-
ducted by Indians to a place where he Saw in Large Masses of many thousands

of pounds weight a Singular Kind of Mineral, it in colour resembles Iron but whiter, it is hard as Steel, Yet [malleable] as gold or silver, it is obedient to the Magnet, but less so than Iron. Neither the Nitric Sulphuric nor Muriatic Accid will touch it, it is not Flexible in the greatest heat that Can be produced in a Blacksmith's furnace, it will neither Corrode nor Rust by exposure to the Atmosphere, it receives a polish as Brilliant as a diamond & of a quicksilver Colour, it is found in a Limestone Country & entirely unmixed with any mineral or other matter. If it is not Platina, I do not know what it is; I have Some of it in my possession & have Sent a piece of it to Philadelphia to be tried. Capt. Glass says an hundred Thousand pounds of it Could be Obtained should it prove Valuable; he Saw several other Curiosities which I find noticed in his Journal which he has permitted me to peruse.—[3]

Finally, wrote Sibley, Glass reported that a war party of one thousand Comanches and Taovaya-Wichitas had embarked that spring for the Arkansas River with the intent of exterminating the Osages, that "common peste to mankind." This had been a common rumor on the southwestern frontier since the days of de Mézières. If an attack on the Three-Forks Osage village did take place, it must have been singularly unsuccessful, for Osage harassment of the Taovaya-Wichitas did not abate.

The role played by the great meteorite of the Southern Plains in early western history has never been examined, but from the present perspective the story intrigues. There existed on this frontier from the time of Coronado's 1541 march in search of Quivira, a long tradition of precious metals stories—particularly ones involving "silver ore" and "silver mines" about the wild rivers of present west-central Texas. La Salle's party of Frenchmen, stranded on the Texas coast in the 1680s, had heard reports of "silver" on the interior rivers, and in 1756 don Bernardo de Miranda reported actually finding solid chunks of what he assumed was silver—"soft like the buckles of shoes"—along the middle Llano River.[4] Virtually all of the American principals on the scene after 1800—William Dunbar, James Wilkinson, Sibley, and Thomas Linnard—heard similar stories from either Indians or hunters and repeated them to the Jefferson administration.[5] As we have seen, several of the Anglo-American trading parties, including Glass's, had taken along mining and assaying equipment in expectation of mining ore.

The instructive thing about the stories is that no silver, except minute traces deep in the fissures of the so-called Central Mineral Re-

gion, has ever been discovered in west-central Texas. What Glass returned with in 1809 were specimens of what, quite likely, had spawned
three generations of "silver ore" rumors among Euroamericans. While
iron-nickel meteorites in Europe had been gathered and hammered
into tools long ago by Neolithic farmers, New World meteorites had
fallen and accumulated without being disturbed for thousands of years.[6]
The evidence is clear that the Indians venerated them, especially
larger ones, and made fetishes and ornaments of them. Glass even saw
arrow points of the substance, according to Linnard. Moreover, tribes
in quest of trade never hesitated to encourage white traders by telling
them what they wanted to hear.

Nor had western science yet grappled with the meteorite as a phenomenon of nature. It was only around 1800 that mineralogists and
chemists in Europe first realized that stones and chunks of iron could
have extraterrestrial origins. A great meteorite shower at L'Aigle,
France, in 1803, had resolved the question of whether such objects
could fall from the skies, but caused general scientific consternation.
Professor Benjamin Silliman, the early nineteenth-century scientist
and pioneer of meteoritics in America, was fortunate enough to ob-
serve a meteorite shower near Weston, Connecticut, in 1807. But in
the *Medical Repository* the following year he was at a loss to explain
the phenomenon, speculating that the pieces may have been thrown
from clouds struck by lightning, or discharged from a volcano—or perhaps had broken off from the moon. Ultimately, the origins of such
objects, Silliman decided, were "inexplicable" to early nineteenth-
century science.[7]

Glass's metal specimens were not silver (they were magnetic); the
only metals to which they bore the slightest resemblance were iron
and, superficially, the precious metal platinum. The most learned man
on the scene, Sibley, suggested the latter, and on May 13 he commissioned Thomas Irwin, former assistant factor at the Natchitoches trading post, to take along a sample to Philadelphia to have it assayed.[8] The
knowledge that a mass of "several thousand pounds" yet lay waiting on
the prairies evidently committed the Indian agent to sponsoring the
next step: an invasion of territory clearly held by Spain in an effort to
procure it.

The Schamp-McCall and Davis Expeditions

A scattering of documents, unfortunately only one (that of a Spanish cavalry officer) firsthand, are extant for piecing together the immediate consequent events. Since their separation from Glass with a portion of the goods in October, 1808, the men who composed his original trading party had returned with their pony herds to Natchitoches and Natchez. Now, fired by the excitement caused by Glass's specimens and by offers of sponsorship, several members of the original Glass party formed rival expeditions to retrieve the mass.[9]

The two existing versions of events surrounding the Schamp-McCall and Davis expeditions of 1809–10 differ in some details, but from them the essential facts may be assembled. What is known is this: almost immediately following Glass's return, in Natchitoches five of the original Glass party (Schamp, McCall, Alexander, Low, and the boy Peter Young—who seemingly had not yet had his fill of the prairies) in company with William McWilliams, Sourdon Dungeon, William Piper, John Smith, and James Corvis, formed a new expedition.[10] Sponsored by several wealthy backers, most prominently Indian Agent John Sibley, this group was outfitted with a sufficient quantity of goods to purchase the meteorite from the Indians, and set out bound for the Taovaya-Wichita villages sometime in June, 1809.[11]

The details of the purchase of Po-a-cat-le-pi-le-car-re from the Indians have not come down to us, only that "Their demands where [*sic*] a certain number of rifles and ammunition and also a quantity of blankets . . ." and that they participated in the retrieval operation, at least at the outset.[12] The willingness of these Indians to sell a major religious shrine to white traders would later evoke some ethnocentric contempt from the young scientific community in America. But it perhaps demonstrates the practical nature of their religion. Clearly, at this point in their fortunes with the well-armed Osages, firearms must have seemed more critical to them. The devastating disease epidemics of 1777 and 1801 also may have eroded their faith in the meteorite's powers, although Glass's journal comments do not really indicate this. And two pieces of the same type of metal, similarly venerated, still remained. Viewed in this context the Indian sale of their healing rock seems pragmatic rather than contemptible. It also illustrates how dependent on the white economy almost all the prairie tribes were, even this early.

The field was becoming crowded, however. Simultaneously with the formation of the well-backed Natchitoches expedition, a second party was being assembled in Natchez.[13] This group was capably guided by veteran plainsman John Davis, also of the original Glass party, and included Aaron Robinson, Edmund Quirk, William Skinner, William McClester, William Knowland, James White, and two or three others.[14] Their plan was to make directly for the meteorite and to steal it while the Natchitoches group was bartering for it on the Red River. No date is given for the departure of the Davis party; probably it was in early summer as well, since a journey that deep into Texas would have taken five to six weeks.

By early autumn of 1809, a third force, one much larger than either of the trading parties, was being mounted in San Antonio de Béxar. After three years of experimentation with their "no noisy disturbances" policy, Spanish officials concluded that they could not allow the Americans to engage in "mining" activity in their territories. Thus Bernardo Bonavía set in motion a major expeditionary force, its objective variously referred to as "against the Americans reported as getting *platina* on the Colorado River," and as an attempt to stop "Anglo-Americans working a mine in the Sierras." Capt. José de Goseascochea, ably seconded by Lieut. Miguel Musquiz (Philip Nolan's conqueror), commanded this fifty-two-man cavalry force, which departed from San Antonio on October 5, 1809.[15]

The chronological sequence and reconstructable details are these. The Davis party was the first to arrive at the location of the meteorite, presumably in July. In their greedy haste they had neglected to provide a means of transporting the mass, which was not only heavy but unwieldy (the original weight of the meteorite was nearly a ton, compressed into an irregular cone forty inches across its base and two feet deep). Temporarily they contented themselves with rolling it away and carefully burying it under a boulder pending their later return. Within a few days the Schamp-McCall party, along with a number of Indians, were astonished upon arriving and finding the meteorite missing. On the second day of looking they nosed it out when someone grasped a clump of grass that pulled up too easily. Using saplings as levers, the party pried the great mass into a horse-drawn wagon and set out for Red River. The going was "very tedious" they told John Maley, particularly after the Indians "left them to do for themselves." Sometime in August, after they had crossed the Brazos to the Grand Prairie, a marauding party of raiders stole their entire remuda. Sibley says Schamp and Piper journeyed on foot to Natchitoches for more; Maley says they went to the Taovaya-Wichita villages and traded two rifles for horses.[16]

By the time this delay had been overcome and (after much "fatigue and trouble") the mass was again en route for the Red River, October must have been well advanced. Goseascochea and Musquiz, meanwhile, had taken the easy and fast route from San Antonio, up the Blackland and Grand prairies to the Tawakoni villages, where they arrived on October 17. Since these were abandoned (a Taovaya told them the inhabitants had already gone west to winter with the Comanches), Goseascochea pushed his force northward, across extensive stretches of burned prairie near present Fort Worth, before swinging west into sierras—the Palo Pinto country. Here they found neither mines nor Americans, and after a week of searching turned back to the Tawakoni villages. Although the Spanish force could not have been more than a month behind the Americans, the only thing the Indians would tell them was that an American from Natchitoches, with nine "Caddos," had been through on a trading voyage to the Taovaya-Wichitas and Comanches. This may have been a garbled account of the Schamp-McCall party, but Goseascochea did not think so and did not investigate. While the Spaniards made their way back to San Antonio, the Americans secured themselves in a camp on the Red River, waiting for a rise so they could float the mass in a canoe built from the trunk of a black walnut tree.[17] After numerous delays and the intricate detour around the Great Raft through the "Great Swamp," they finally arrived in Natchitoches on June 4, 1810.[18]

For nearly a year Natchitoches seethed with excitement over its resident curiosity. "Scientists" and would-be miners scrutinized it and blacksmiths tried their craft on it. Repeatedly it was rung like a bell by striking it with a metal object. Maley asserts that during the several months of the mass's residence in Natchitoches, small fortunes were offered to the hunter-traders for their shares, but all were refused.[19] Finally, the mass was consigned to a New Orleans merchant named James Johnston for shipping to New York to have it tested and assayed. McCall and Holmes accompanied it down the Mississippi and then returned to Natchitoches anxiously to await the outcome. Within a year Sibley relayed word to them that the object had turned out to be "iron" and thus was valueless. The hunter-trader element at once distrusted Sibley; in fact, judging from other evidence, the men who had retrieved the meteorite never gave up the idea that the masses were valuable. The early American geographer William Darby, who was in Natchitoches during the period, spoke with two of them and has left us this comment: "the persons engaged were in general too ignorant to understand the decisive results of such tests, and unwilling to abandon a pleasing delusion; and the Cabinet of science stands indebted to their infatuation for its possession." [20]

The summer, fall, and winter of 1809–10 produced by way of Spanish response a major flurry of activity to stop contraband trading penetrations by the Americans. It began in August with an expedition financed from the *mesteño* fund (money raised from the capture and sale of mustangs) to drive "undesirables" from the Neutral Ground, and continued with the Goseascochea-Musquiz expedition to halt illegal "mining." Additionally, that October Nicolás Benítez was dispatched to the *ranchería* of Comanche chief Hunchinampa to investigate rumors that American mustangers were residing there. As other reports came in that winter—of two Americans gathering horses and mules on the Sabine, of another trading for mustangs among the Taovayas that fall—Texas governor Manuel Salcedo took about the only actions possible on such a lightly held frontier. He sent word to Guadiana at Nacogdoches to investigate and attempt to intercept any American expedition entering Texas, and again encouraged Marcel Soto to divert as much trade as possible to Bayou Pierre, an impossible task for that trader because of a dearth of goods. Additionally, Barr and Davenport sent two traders, Pedro Engle and Nicolás Pont, to the Tawakonis and the Taovaya-Wichitas in 1809. Finally, in January of 1810, Salcedo addressed representatives of the North Texas tribes, presenting them with gifts, appealing for their loyalty, and promising to protect them from the Osages. There was little else he could do. [21]

The Passing of the Old Order

The year 1810 was a watershed in the early American push onto the Southern Plains. Although Spanish officials continued to be alarmed about contraband mustanging (the Spanish minister to the United States, Luis de Onís, warned Texas Governor Salcedo not to relax on the issue, for example), after 1810 the complaints largely involved mustangers operating closer to Louisiana—along the Sabine and Sulphur, in Caddo lands. One of the reasons the documents dealing with traders melt away after 1810 is because of the preoccupation on both sides of the border with Father Hidalgo's long-expected *revolución*, which broke out in Mexico that year. Many Anglo-Americans who once might have made long trips to the prairies to trade and mustang in the post-1810 age joined filibuster parties and invaded Texas.[22]

Another reason was the sudden death of the Taovaya leader, Awahakei, in 1811—an event which, disturbingly for the Plains Caddoans, seemed to have been presaged by the appearance of the Great Comet of 1811 in the night skies of northern Texas. Traditionally they regarded such phenomena as serious omens; later anthropologists recorded that they associated meteor showers and comets with the end of the world, and some twentieth-century groups retained the idea that "when the stars fly around, great leaders will die."[23] The 1811 combination of events, coming as they did in the wake of the sale of the meteorite to the whites, seems to have plunged the villages into dissent and controversy. That year the Red River villages broke up, rather than elect a new chief, and small groups of Taovayas, Wichitas, Skidis, and Iscanis scattered across the southern prairies. For fifty-five years this village complex had been the most important Euroamerican trade base on the Southern Plains, and its disintegration deprived the Americans of their most important Indian contacts there.

During the same period the opposition suffered a setback of its own. The Nacogdoches trading house of Barr and Davenport, straining ever since Sibley had cut off their supply of Natchitoches goods late in 1808, dissolved for practical purposes with William Barr's death in 1810. For two more years Samuel Davenport carried on a half-hearted struggle to locate items in Pensacola for the Spanish Indian trade. But in 1812 he finally turned his back on Spain, joining the revolutionary Gutiérrez-Magee filibuster that invaded Texas that year.[24] The experience of this frontier trading house points up the salient problem faced by Spain in its competition for Indian allies: with a relatively under-developed manufacturing system at home, Spanish officials throughout the empire were continually forced to obtain trade goods from other nations. It was an arrangement that not only was subject to interruption, but also opened Spain to being undersold, especially when the source of goods was also her competition in the trade.

All these events served to define and separate the change to a new era. The old order had been a continuation—considerable parties of Natchitoches and Natchez hunters patterning their routes, trade policies, and alliances along lines already established for them by the French. But these well-outfitted excursions declined after the return of Schamp and McCall in 1810, so much so that by 1813 Sibley began to depend upon the Caddo chief, Dehahuit, rather than traders to deal with the interior tribes. In 1817 the U.S. factory was moved several hundred miles upriver, to the mouth of the Sulphur River, in order to accommodate trade demands in the absence of sizeable trading expeditions.[25] Scholars have unearthed material from farther north, on the central plains, on at least seven large American trading expeditions launched from Saint Louis toward Santa Fe between 1810 and 1821. But south of the Canadian, Hispanic Comancheros from New Mexico seem to have taken over much Comanche trade of this decade, while Glass's "Owaheys"—the Skidi Pawnee middlemen—remained the chief source of guns for Texas Indians.[26] In 1819 the United States even relinquished Jefferson's aggressive claim to Texas in the Adams-Onís Treaty of that year, only to see Mexico win its independence two years later, and both Texas and New Mexico soon opened to American traders, and even colonists. The days of American traders sneaking secret messages and United States flags to the Texas tribes, and skulking and hiding from Spanish patrols, was over.

Anthony Glass, 1810–1819

Little is known of the subsequent life of Anthony Glass. Whether it was greater sagacity in such matters or merely a disinclination for further wandering on the great prairies, Glass did not take part in the retrieval of the meteorite. He must have seen a more substantial future in ginning cotton for his neighbors and building up and acting as overseer of his family's growing estate—a choice of occupation many of the other hunters perhaps did not enjoy. Although he seems never to have remarried, Anthony did remain close to his brother, who helped him raise his children and who named a son born in 1807 after him. No record exists of Anthony Glass's death, but family tradition places the date in 1819, and in 1822 Sibley told Benjamin Silliman, referring to the journal, that "Capt. Glass who kept it has been dead Several years." Following the death of his brother Andrew Glass in 1823, the family estate passed into the hands of the younger generation: Anthony's son, James Glass, and Andrew's son, Anthony, who died in 1834. By the time of the Civil War, James Glass was comfortably situated on lands built up by his father and uncle—the Glass properties in Mississippi were then assessed at eighty-five thousand dollars.[27]

Glass's journal has a more traceable history than the man himself. The original was turned over to Sibley upon Glass's arrival in Natchitoches in 1809, the Indian agent's intent at the time to forward it to the War Department. But perhaps because his own implication in contraband trade on Spanish soil was too obvious, Sibley decided not to trust the journal to new Secretary of War William Eustis. For two or three years he did show it to important figures who visited Natchitoches and who were interested in southwestern geography. One individual who perused it was former explorer Zebulon M. Pike, dispatched to Natchitoches in 1811 to clear "human driftwood" from the Neutral Ground, who was then preparing his own report on the Southwest for publication. More important, Sibley also showed the Glass journal to geographer William Darby, who found it an "honestly written" account, and through whom some of Glass's descriptions found their way into the maps of the day. Both Darby's "Map of the United States Including Louisiana" (1818) and John Melish's "United States" (1818, 1822, 1824) substantially incorporate Glass's version of the origins and courses of the Colorado, Brazos, Trinity, Sulphur, and Sabine rivers.[28]

American Science and the "Texas Iron"

For nearly a decade the Glass journal lay forgotten in a trunk in Sibley's home before becoming the object of an intense search by Professor Benjamin Silliman of Yale University. Since witnessing the 1807 Connecticut meteorite shower, Silliman increasingly had become fascinated with meteorites. Along with the rest of the scientific community he was startled in 1814 when *Bruce's American Mineralogical Journal* reported the results of an analysis in New York of a huge mass of metal that had been named the "Louisiana Iron." Although the tests confirmed that the metal was an iron alloy containing no precious metals, its weight—reported as "upwards of three thousand pounds"—stunned scientists who believed they knew what the mass was.[29] One such was Col. George Gibbs, a mineralogist who had had some experience with the L'Aigle meteorites in France. Recognizing the mass as very likely a gigantic meteorite—by far the largest ever collected up to that time— Gibbs purchased it just before it was to be shipped to Europe and sold as a New World curiosity—an idea Sibley had promoted as early as 1812. Shortly thereafter Silliman confirmed Gibbs's suspicions when his own examination disclosed that the malleable property of the mass was caused by the presence of nickel.[30]

Because of its size, the Louisiana Iron (or Texas Iron, as it was renamed once the details of its discovery and retrieval became known) was of great interest to scientists in both America and Europe. Silliman published numerous accounts of his experiments with it in the fledgling *American Journal of Science and Arts*. Benjamin Silliman, Jr., T. S. Hunt, and Charles U. Shepard continued to study it and to publish notices about it for half a century.[31] Their tests proved it to be what is now called a siderite, an iron-nickel–alloy meteorite, composed of 90.02 percent iron and 9.67 percent nickel. Internally it consisted of a series of octahedronally positioned plates that in cross section displayed a pattern known as Widmanstätten figures (which confirmed a theory regarding the internal structure of iron meteorites first advanced in 1808). An early photoengraving of the meteorite's medium octahedrite pattern was published in an 1846 article on it. Since both Indians and traders described it as being little embedded, it probably was a direct-motion meteorite, falling at low velocity between midnight and noon in the direction of the earth's spin.[32] Several pieces had already been broken off, but Silliman contrived a way to weigh it that yielded 1,635 pounds, considerably less than the estimates.

As the prize meteorite in the world at the time, the circumstances of the discovery of the mass seemed worthy of investigation, and in the early 1820s the elder Silliman set about collecting them. From William Darby he learned of the existence of the journal (although

Darby recollected that the author's name had been "Holmes"); in 1822 he finally secured the extant, copied version, which appears here, from Sibley. Evidently Sibley believed the journal was going to be published, for he took the liberty of having his young copyist insert the "Song of the Orphan" folk tradition and the appended "Character of the Hietan Indians."

Silliman also uncovered one other prize document that considerably illuminates the meteorite's impact on the frontier mind. During a chance conversation about the famed mass in 1821, Silliman had discovered from Supreme Court Justice William Johnson of Charleston that there existed yet another individual who claimed to have had firsthand experience with the remaining meteorites mentioned by the Indians, and who had also kept a journal. Johnson related the story this way: "The Man from whom I received my Information was named Maley. He was thrown my Way by Accident & finding that he was one of those troubled Spirits that find Rest only in Motion, I elicited from him a number of the Incidents of a Life spent in Wandering. But among the things I well remember that he said he had kept a Journal of his Adventures in the Western Country, which he had sold to a Bookseller in New-York for five hundred Dollars."[33]

Some digging on Silliman's part produced the Maley "Journal," a 180-page manuscript purchased by one Isaac Riley but never published because of the collapse of Riley's publishing house in the Panic of 1819.[34]

Almost nothing is known about John Maley, except that he wrote a "journal" which shares some characteristics with two more famous accounts of the early West—James Ohio Pattie's *Personal Narrative* and David Coyner's *The Lost Trappers*—which scholars now regard as semi-fictitious. We know that John Maley was a real person and not a nom de plume, but he does not appear in any of the U.S. censuses between 1790 and 1820, an explainable but troubling fact. His story is certainly an entertaining one, and in some ways useful.[35] Despite the firsthand posture of the account, Maley's information respecting the meteorite, and almost all other details of trader life in the Southwest, seem actually to have been secondhand, derived from a close grilling of the hunter-traders in Natchitoches during a visit there sometime between 1810 and 1812. Written several years after the fact, with a melodramatic sense of adventure (at one point he nearly dies of thirst on the Blackland Prairie), the Maley journal has some utility as a secondhand

report from the frontier, whose perceptions of the events in the Southwest from 1808 to 1812 mirror those of the trader-hunter element. His
account does describe, with an accuracy corroborated by other sources,
the expeditions of 1809–10, as told to him by several members of the
Schamp-McCall party. It also includes purported journal entries from
two trading voyages Maley claimed to have made onto the plains in
1812 and 1813. On these expeditions (the details of which he possibly
obtained by interviewing an actual trader) he wrote of being shown one
of the remaining meteorites, contracting to buy it, but being robbed of
his goods by the Osages, and of discovering an abandoned Spanish
mining works in northern Texas.

Perhaps what the Maley document really indicates is the intensity
of the excitement on the frontier over these masses of metal. The effect
lingered on for many years. As late as 1824, several Anglo colonists in
Texas, led by a "Judge Duke" who had struck up a conversation "with a
man by the name of Scamp" in Natchitoches in 1819, were contemplat-
ing a penetration of the Comanchería in search of the remaining masses.
Only the untimely death of their guide, "old Comanche trader" William
McWilliams (on the expedition with Schamp that retrieved the original mass) caused the foray to be called off.[36] One wonders, in fact, if the
real substance behind Jim Bowie's fabled "Lost Silver Mine" of west-
central Texas does not actually spring from the imprint left by these
meteorites on the minds of the next southwestern-frontier generation,
from which Bowie sprang.

Po-a-cat-le-pi-le-car-re was in 1829 transferred to the Lyceum of
Natural History in New York, and after Gibb's death in 1833 was presented by his widow to the Cabinet of Mineralogy at Yale. In 1877 it
was turned over to the Peabody Museum of Natural History, where it
now resides as the prize specimen in that museum's historic meteorite
collection. Today the former healing shrine of the Southern Plains
tribes is known as "Red River." It remains the largest existing find from
Texas and the seventh-largest preserved meteorite from North America.[37] The remaining pieces mentioned by Glass have their own history.
Indian artist George Catlin evidently painted one of the remaining
"Medicine Rocks" during his first visit to the Southwest in 1834, showing a mass which appears to have been placed in an upright position
atop a ledge of rock. Not until 1856, however, was a large iron meteorite from the area finally retrieved. That piece, a coarse octahedrite

Apparently this unpublished Catlin oil, called "Comanches giving the arrows to the Medicine Rock," portrays the Neighbors meteorite, now in the University of Texas Museum. (Courtesy National Museum of American Art, Smithsonian Institution)

obtained by Robert S. Neighbors, Indian agent for the Brazos Reservation, weighed some 320 pounds. Neighbors (who is the source of the Comanche term for a fallen meteorite) described it as "a regular metior" and "a beautiful specimine" and reported that the Comanches made offerings to it and sought cures by rubbing their bodies against it. Their strong protests against its removal were ignored; today the piece that remains of the "Neighbors" or "Wichita County" meteorite is on exhibit in the Texas Memorial Museum at the University of Texas at Austin. It is the second largest in the museum's collection of more than four thousand meteorites.[38] In the twentieth century other iron meteorites have been found near the spot where Glass and his party first saw "Red River" in 1808, and one—the forty-five-pound Comanche County meteorite discovered in the area in 1940—may be the third piece.[39]

A Forgotten Frontier

Were it not for these masses, we probably would not now be able to reconstruct many of the details of this early phase of trader history in the Southwest, but the events explored here transcend the natural history of any meteorite. Masses of metal—like mustangs or beaver pelts— were only objects of booty to men who sought to divert the wealth of the wilderness into their pockets. Fired by the most speculative of capitalist drives, the packtrain traders of the Texas wilderness—Nolan, House, Lewis and Alexander, Davis, Glass, and Schamp—represented the cutting edge of an expanding American culture first contacting an entrenched, and alarmed, Hispanic culture of a century's residence in that part of the world. In many ways the Americans only inherited the imperial struggle for this land, but they also found themselves, for a time, the executors of a government policy of expansion that otherwise had been frustrated. In truth they were, as James Wilkinson warned Spanish New World officials in his famous "Reflections on Louisiana" letter of 1804, "adventurous desperadoes . . . like the ancient Goths and Vandals," whose activities and explorations would if unchecked give the key to the New World to Spain's "most dangerous neighbor and [to] the revolutionary spirit of the present time."[40]

Less than half a century was required to sound the full implications of Wilkinson's warning.

Notes

Part 1. Introduction

1. Statement by one of the [Nolan] party, in Donald Jackson, ed., *The Journals of Zebulon Montgomery Pike, with Letters and Related Documents*, II, 256.

2. Zebulon M. Pike to the *Herald*, Natchitoches, July 22, 1807, printed in the Natchez *Herald*, August 18, 1807.

3. A complete bibliographic essay on this topic is unnecessary. Suffice it to say that the best works covering the American frontier in the early Southwest, those of Mattie Austin Hatcher (*The Opening of Texas to Foreign Settlement, 1801–1821*) and Isaac Joslin Cox ("The Louisiana-Texas Frontier"), now approach three-quarters of a century in age and despite their high quality are now in need of updating and revision. The works of professors Herbert Eugene Bolton, John Francis McDermott, Jack Holmes, and Abraham Nasatir are, of course, first-rate, but have focused primarily upon the Spanish or French periods and perspectives. A recent reinterpretation of the early American frontier in the Southwest appears in Dan Flores, ed., *Jefferson and Southwestern Exploration: The Freeman and Custis Accounts of the Red River Expedition of 1806*. We are soon to be treated to a new coverage of this period, also, in the sequel to Elizabeth A. H. John's *Storms Brewed in Other Men's Worlds: The Confrontation of Indians, Spanish, and French in the Southwest, 1540–1795*.

4. Howard R. Lamar, *The Trader on the American Frontier: Myth's Victim*, 40. Lamar's revisionist stance contrasts sharply with that of earlier historians. Carl C. Rister, who focuses on a later period in his "Harmful Practices of Indian Traders of the Southwest, 1865–1876," *New Mexico Historical Quarterly* 6 (July, 1931): 231–48, cites the traders for exploiting and cheating the Indians, selling them whiskey and guns, and lays a large portion of the blame for Texas border warfare on them—"the jetsam of the turbulent sea of border life" (p. 232). See also Andy J. Middlebrooks and Glenna Middlebrooks, "Holland Coffee of Red River," *Southwestern Historical Quarterly* 69 (October, 1965): 145–62. Richard Slotkin, in *Regeneration through Violence: The Mythology of the American Frontier, 1600–1860*, 551–57, sees the frontier "hunter-wastrel" who manned most of the trading expeditions as the executor of wilderness destruction couched in romantic terms, a subtle and pervasive symbol of the continual extension of American influence into new areas. Ethnohistorians add that traders were instrumental in the economic (hence cultural) transformation of Indian cultures. It is an unending debate.

5. The quote is from Athanase de Mézières, the Natchitoches Frenchman who, as director of North Texas trade during the Spanish regime of the 1770s, endeavored to win over the *norteños*. See Athanase de Mézières to Theodoro Croix, Taovayas Villages, April 18, 1778, in Herbert E. Bolton, ed., *Athanase de Mézières and the Louisiana-Texas Frontier, 1768–1780*, II, 201–204.

Scholars list today nine different historic Southern Plains Caddoans bands recorded in the sources. Fragmentation and deculturation have now brought all the descendants under the collective term "Wichita," the Europeanized rendering of the name of an important band. See Alexander Lesser, "Caddoan Kinship Systems," *Nebraska His-

tory 60 (1979): 260–71. Americans during the period under study attempted the Indian names (what the Spaniards heard as "Taovayas" sounded to American ears like "Towiache" or "Toweeach"), but usually called all these peoples "Panis." While recognizing and where appropriate indicating the other clans and bands present at the Red River villages, in this work I generally refer to the complex of peoples as Taovaya-Wichitas, a term of convenience.

6. J. Frank Dobie, *The Mustangs*; and two articles by Francis Haines, "Where Did the Plains Indians Get Their Horses?" and "The Northward Spread of Horses among the Plains Indians," both in *American Anthropologist* 40 (1938): 112–17, 429–37. Astonishingly, a recent work on the horse still perpetuates the myth—thoroughly discredited in the above works—that the wild horse of the West was descended from animals escaped from the Coronado and De Soto expeditions. See John Clabby, *The Natural History of the Horse*, 56–57.

7. Isaac J. Cox, ed., "Memoir by the Sieur De La Tonty," in *The Journeys of René Robert Cavelier Sieur De La Salle*, II, 47–48.

8. The Frenchmen who traversed East Texas in the 1680s saw no wild horses, but the de León and Terán expeditions of 1689–91 brought more than 1,000 horses and mules into the region, at least 200 of which were lost (Dobie, *Mustangs*, 97–98).

9. Francis Haines, *Horses In America*, pp. 93–95; Heather Smith Thomas, *The Wild Horse Controversy*, 30. John Sibley asserts that in 1802 an estimated 7,300 Texas horses passed through Louisiana to eastern markets (Sibley to Orleans Territorial Gov. W. C. C. Claiborne, Natchitoches, October 10, 1803, in Clarence Carter and John P. Bloom, comps. and eds., *The Territorial Papers of the United States*, IX, 75). On occasion an exceptional Indian pony, usually a paint stud, would bring much more, but on the whole mustangs were cheap compared to American stock. According to ads in the *Mississippi Messenger* (Natchez) in 1807, American stock of similar size (13½ hands) in good condition brought $45 to $80.

The northern and eastern ranges of wild horses in the West at the turn of the nineteenth century were fixed by the American explorers of the day. Lewis and Clark saw no wild horses on the Northern Plains during their 1804–1806 expedition. Pike, however, frequently sighted bands along the Arkansas River in 1806 and saw "immense herds" in South Texas in 1807. Freeman and Custis, whose 1806 expedition was stopped about a week short of the Blackland Prairies, do not mention wild horses at all in the woods and bottoms of Arkansas and Texas.

10. On Natchez and West Florida, and the movement of Americans into the area, see Robert V. Haynes, *The Natchez District and the American Revolution*, and Isaac J. Cox, *The West Florida Controversy, 1798–1813*.

11. See Noel M. Loomis, "Philip Nolan's Entry in Texas in 1800," in John F. McDermott, ed., *The Spanish in the Mississippi Valley, 1762–1804*, 120–33; Noel Loomis and Abraham Nasatir, *Pedro Vial and the Roads to Santa Fe*, chap. 9. Except where otherwise indicated, the following treatment of Nolan draws heavily upon these two works.

12. Dunbar to Jefferson, Natchez, August 22, 1801; Clark to Jefferson, New Orleans, February 12, 1799, both in "[Documents] Concerning Philip Nolan," *Quarterly of the Texas State Historical Association* (April, 1904): 315, 310.

13. The quote is in Nolan to Pedro de Nava, San Antonio, November 25, 1797, tomo 413, Sección de Historia, Archivo General y Público, Mexico City Document no. 8, reproduced in Lawrence Kinnaird, "American Penetration into Spanish Louisiana," in Herbert Eugene Bolton, comp., *New Spain and the Anglo American West:*

Historical Contributions Submitted to Herbert Eugene Bolton, I, 236. The Taovaya-Wichitas and other tribes beyond the Caddos were declared off-limits to Natchitoches traders in "Notice to the Public," Natchitoches, June 24, 1788 (in Lawrence Kinnaird, ed., *Spain in the Mississippi Valley, 1765–1794* II, 256). The Pennsylvania Irishmen—Barr, Murphy, and Davenport—had all become naturalized citizens of New Spain prior to the turn of the century. They had obtained exclusive rights to supply the East Texas and surrounding tribes—commonly with American goods purchased in Natchitoches—in 1798. From 1800 on they drove large herds of horses and mules to West Florida. For a history of their venture, see J. Villasana Haggard, "The House of Barr and Davenport," *Southwestern Historical Quarterly* 49 (July, 1945): 65–88.

14. Nolan to Wilkinson, Frankfort, June 10, 1796, in James Wilkinson, *Memoirs Of My Own Times*, II, appendix 2.

15. Ellicott met Nolan at the mouth of the Wabash River in January of 1797. Finding that he could obtain from him "much useful information" and that "he had a very extensive knowledge of that country, particularly Louisiana," Ellicott invited Nolan to descend the Mississippi with their party (it included future Jeffersonian explorer Thomas Freeman) during that January and February (Andrew Ellicott, *The Journal of Andrew Ellicott*, 29–37).

16. Nolan to Wilkinson, New Orleans, April 24, 1797; Wilkinson, *Memoirs* II, appendix 2.

17. The source of the quote on Nolan's 1797 expedition is Nolan to Wilkinson, Natchez, July 21, 1797, in *Memoirs*. On the maps, see Wilkinson to Aaron Burr, New York, March 26, 1804: "call upon me at one o'clock and see my Maps," in the Papers of Aaron Burr, Series I, Correspondence, the New-York Historical Society. Also, Wilkinson to Dearborn, July 13, 1804, War Department, Letters Received, Main Series, National Archives Record Group M222, wherein Wilkinson asserts that the maps were based upon Nolan's travels. According to the editors of the Burr Papers, this untitled, professionally drafted map of Louisiana-Texas is the only extant map of the group. Donald Jackson concurs with me on the map's provenance and speculates that Sergeant Anthony Nau, cartographer in Wilkinson's command, may have helped draft it. The original is in the Houghton Library, Harvard University, Cambridge, Massachusetts.

18. The quotes are from Wilkinson to Dearborn, July 13, 1804, War Department, a twenty-two page manuscript, yet unpublished, that provided the Jefferson administration with its most complete account of the Spanish Southwest. From other corroborating evidence, Nolan seems to have made the journey disclosing these discoveries during his initial expedition, probably during the years 1791–92.

19. Historians have long puzzled over this question. Some scholars seem to think Nolan was dead when Jefferson's letter arrived; Loomis says there was an interview, but how could it have been in 1799? I believe I can lay the problem of a Nolan-Jefferson meeting to rest with the following documents from the Thomas Jefferson Papers, Library of Congress Manuscripts Division, listed chronologically, as I have used them here: Jefferson to Nolan, Philadelphia, June 24, 1798; Jefferson to Dunbar, Philadelphia, January 16, 1800; Wilkinson to Jefferson, Fort Adams, May 22, 1800 [letter of introduction for Nolan]; Clark to Jefferson, New Orleans, May 29, 1800; Wilkinson to Jefferson, Washington, September 1, 1800. In this last Wilkinson writes that he was certain "that Mr. N. would have presented Himself to you long before this period, but a Letter which I have received from Kentucky has induced a contrary apprehension." Jefferson did receive Wilkinson's letter introducing Nolan (the creases where it was folded in Nolan's pocket are still visible), delivered by messenger on November 3—two days after Nolan had crossed

the Mississippi for the last time. It was not a good year for authority figures in Nolan's life, and Jefferson had to hear of the young trader's discoveries secondhand, through Wilkinson and Dunbar.

20. Pedro de Nava to Don de Berenguer, November 25, 1800, cited in Loomis and Nasatir, *Pedro Vial*, 213.

21. See Nolan to Jesse Cook, Natchez, October 21, 1800, quoted in its entirety in Loomis and Nasatir, *Pedro Vial*, 217–18; "Memoir of Colonel Ellis P. Bean," in Henderson K. Yoakum, *History of Texas* . . . , I, app. 2. I make no attempt to treat the full Spanish response or the range of documents, since the Spanish side of Nolan's last foray is closely reconstructed by Loomis and Nasatir, as well as others.

22. Lamar, *Trader on the Frontier*, 16. Traders invited the wrath of more puritanical contemporaries within "polite society" by participating in the freer sexual lifestyle of the Indian communities, with Indian women who frequently were perceived by white women in the settlements as rivals. The best recent work on the topic is by Sylvia Van Kirk, *"Many Tender Ties": Women in Fur-Trade Society, 1670–1870.*

23. Lewis O. Saum, *The Fur Trader and the Indian*, 3. These early leaders of trading expeditions may have been prototypes of William Goetzmann's trapper "Jacksonian capitalists." Goetzmann's hypothesis, along with others, is critically examined in Harvey Lewis Carter and Marcia Carpenter Spencer, "Stereotypes of the Mountain Man," *Western Historical Quarterly* 6 (January, 1975): 17–32.

24. Zebulon Pike, embarrassed by some of the actions of Nolan's imprisoned companions, explained to Spanish officials that "they are most of them very illiterate, and possessing scarcely any part of an education," (Pike to Salcedo, Chihuahua, April 4, 1807, in Jackson, *Journals of Pike*, II, 171).

25. Dan Flores, ed., "The John Maley Journal: Travels and Adventures in the American Southwest, 1810–1813," master's thesis, Northwestern State University, Natchitoches, 1972, 38–40. Maley's experience is an example of how trader-hunters actively resisted civilization's advance on the Indian lands. The changes were repugnant to the interests of both. Peter Custis, the young naturalist of Jefferson's Red River expedition, had less difficulty obtaining information from "the best and most respectable hunters and traders," but was somewhat suspicious of it. When they described "herds" of "White wolves" and "Ten thousand [bison] at a sight," he believed they exaggerated. Although he thought the landmark chart he obtained from them was topographically accurate, he felt obliged to reduce all mileage estimates by a third. See Custis's "Natural History Catalogues" and "Landmark Chart" in Flores, *Jefferson and Southwestern Exploration*, 272, 274, appendix 2.

26. The principal document on Chalvert (Calvert) is de Nava to Alcudia, Chihuahua, November 3, 1795, cited in Loomis and Nasatir, *Pedro Vial*, 171–72 (see also pp. 412, 426). By 1805 Calvert was working for Spain and went along as interpreter with Pedro Vial in the expedition to persuade the Pawnees to attack Lewis and Clark.

27. The sole extant document on Sanders is a letter from Edwin Turner to W. C. C. Claiborne, Natchitoches, July 16, 1804, in Dunbar Rowland, ed., *Official Letter-Books of W. C. C. Claiborne, 1801–1816*, II, 31–33. In 1802 there were two Sanderses— Joseph and James—who signed a squatter's petition circulated in the Natchez area (Petition to Congress by Citizens of the Territory, [August 25, 1802], in Carter and Bloom, *Territory of Mississippi*, V, 162, 167).

28. J. F. H. Claiborne, *Mississippi As a Province, Territory and State, with Biographical Notices of Eminent Citizens*, 152–53, notes. Since Ashley was a friend of Nolan's, it is not surprising to note that he seems to have been one of James Wilkinson's

agents in the border country during the great conspiracy of 1806. Ashley's political sympathies were consistent; when Aaron Burr escaped from Washington, Mississippi Territory, in February of 1807, it was with Ashley's assistance (Thomas Perkins Abernethy, *The Burr Conspiracy*, 219, 223).

29. The Spanish letters are Salcedo to Bautista, Chihuahua, January 2, 1804; Bautista to Salcedo, San Antonio, January 4, 1804; José Joaquín Ugarte to Bautista, Nacogdoches, February 9, 1804; Bautista to Salcedo, San Antonio, April 25, 1804, all in the Bexar Archives, Barker Texas History Center, University of Texas at Austin.

30. Davis seems to have been a wandering son of the Davis family of the Walnut Hills area (the site of present Vicksburg), a family that had settled near the Glass family and that was considered "in culture and means far ahead of the usual class of pioneers" (Claiborne, *Mississippi As a Province*, 534—35). Davis probably had long known Anthony Glass and may have been a major source of information on "silver mines" in the Taovayas country. He will accompany the Glass expedition and lead a third foray to haul back the Texas Iron meteorite in 1809.

31. The Spanish letters on the Davis and Dauni expedition are Ugarte to Bautista, Nacogdoches, June 3, 1804; Bautista to Salcedo, San Antonio, June 20, 1804; Dionisio Valle to Bautista, Nacogdoches, October 3, 1805; Cordero to Salcedo, San Antonio, November 24, 1805, the Bexar Archives.

32. Biographical details are from Julia Kathryn Garrett's introduction in her fine documents collection, "Doctor John Sibley and the Louisiana-Texas Frontier, 1803—1814," *Southwestern Historical Quarterly* 45 (January, 1942): 286—92; and G. P. Whittington's introduction to his Sibley collection, "Dr. John Sibley Of Natchitoches, 1757—1837," *Louisiana Historical Quarterly* 10 (October, 1927): 467—73.

33. Sibley studied Dehahuit closely over a decade, and from his letters and other documents a picture emerges of a man with a strong mind, kind and judicious, and a leader whose people's long and rewarding bicultural relationship with the French had engendered in him a great respect for the whites. Complaints by Spanish frontier officials against "El Doctor Sikbley" and his activities among Dehahuit and the border Indians even reached Havana and Madrid. See Cordero to Caso Calvo, San Antonio, September 11, 1805, in Papeles procedentes de la Isla de Cuba, Archivo General de Indias, Madrid, Southwest Collection, Texas Tech University, Lubbock.

34. Cordero to Salcedo, San Antonio, November 24, 1805, the Bexar Archives. Additional letters on the House expedition are Valle to Bautista, Nacogdoches, March 22 and May 4, 1805. The Spanish action in this case was to send a thirty-man patrol down the Red River from the Taovaya-Wichita villages in the fall of 1805, with the purpose of driving back all Anglo-American parties.

35. Details and documentation for this interpretation, as well as information on leaders and objectives for Jefferson's second major Louisiana probe, are in the introduction to Flores, *Jefferson and Southwestern Exploration*, 23—24, 46, 49—61, 75—84.

36. Dunbar to Dearborn, Natchez, March 18 and May 6, 1806, in Eron Dunbar Rowland, comp., *Life, Letters and Papers of William Dunbar*, 332, 341.

37. Jefferson to Thomas Freeman, Esquire, Monticello, April 14, 1804. The original is in the Thomas Jefferson Papers; Freeman's carefully preserved copy is in the Peter Force Collection, Manuscripts Division, Library of Congress. The letter has now been published, in its entirety, in Flores, *Jefferson and Southwestern Exploration*, appendix 1. Freeman's private dinner with the president took place on November 16, 1805.

38. Flores, *Jefferson and Southwestern Exploration*, introduction; John Sibley, "Historical Sketches of the Several Tribes in Louisiana South of the Arkansas River and

between the Mississippi and the River Grand." "Historical Sketches" and the journal section of Sibley's "1805 Report" are widely available, most readily in *Annals of Congress*, 9th Cong., 2nd sess. (1806), 1076–1106.

39. Custis's quote and details here are from Flores, *Jefferson and Southwestern Exploration*, 174 and editor's introduction. My discussion of the objectives for the Melgares expedition, a topic of much debate among scholars of early Western exploration, appears on p. 125 n. 5 of this work. Melgares's subsequent route has also produced questions, all of which are brought on by the loss of the journal he certainly kept. Although Melgares was ordered to the Red River to capture Freeman and Custis, the supposition (since Vial's travels really hadn't cleared the Spanish mind on southwestern geography) that this river headed in the Sangre de Cristos led him instead to the upper Canadian. (Two years later Francisco Amangual crossed the Llano Estacado from Tierra Blanca Draw to "the Red River," only to be told by a man who had been with Melgares in 1806 that, yes, this bigger river was called "Colorado," but it emptied into the "Nepestle" [the Arkansas]. The draw he had just left, Amangual was told, was the source of the "Natchitoches" river.) It seems that Melgares descended the Canadian, but discovered upon treating with a Comanche band that he was not on the river the Americans were exploring; he may also have learned that Viana had met them on July 28. He then struck out overland to treat with the Pawnees on the Arkansas, but first met a group of Skidis. It was probably from this group that Melgares took away the ten-year-old son of Chalvert or Calvert, and at some point among the Pawnees he arrested two Frenchmen and one Nicolas Cole. The information is from Juan Real Alencaster to Nemicio Salcedo, Santa Fe, October 8, 1806, the Spanish Archives of New Mexico, Southwest Collection, Texas Tech University, Lubbock. See, also, Donald Nuttall's "The American Threat to New Mexico, 1804–1822" (master's thesis, San Diego State College, 1959), wherein it is argued (pp. 79–83) that the last described events took place at the Taovaya-Wichita location on the Red River.

40. The most scholarly and useful study of the Neutral Ground is J. Villasana Haggard, "The Neutral Ground between Louisiana and Texas, 1806–1821," *Louisiana Historical Quarterly* 28 (October, 1945): 1001–1128.

41. Cordero to N. Salcedo, San Antonio, February 4, 1807; Salcedo to Cordero, Chihuahua, July 12, 1807; Cordero to Viana, San Antonio, November 3, 1807, the Bexar Archives.

42. At least four of these men were squatters in the Natchez area at the time of their trading-hunting expedition. According to Sibley, Lewis was originally from Kentucky; in 1809 he appears in the lists of squatters east of the Pearl River. Alexander was of a family influential in politics in North Carolina, and was an "ingenuous friendly man" who became a favorite with the Taovayas. By 1802 he was squatting near the Glass family, and will act as one of Glass's guides in 1808. Downs, Watkins, and Lusk were from squatter families in the same area. John Litton may have been from Natchez in 1806, but in 1825 he was living on Bayou San Miguel in western Natchitoches Parish. Joseph Lucas, the interpreter, seems to have been a métis with some Caddoan ancestry. He had served as a guide for Freeman and Custis (who referred to him by his Caddo name, "Talapoon"), and will accompany Glass on the 1808–1809 expedition. Sibley reported in 1811 that one "Lucas" was living at Pecan Point, the white-black-Indian banditti community on the Red River. Sources on the identities of these are Sibley to Dearborn, Natchitoches, July 3, 1807, in Garrett, "Doctor John Sibley" 45 (April, 1942): 381; John Sibley, *A Report from Natchitoches in 1807*, Annie Heloise Abel, ed., entry for June 25, 1807, p. 40; in Carter and Bloom, *Territory of Mississippi*, V, Petition to Congress by Citizens of the

Territory, [August 25, 1802], 161, 168, 169, 171, and Petition to Congress by Inhabitants East of Pearl River, [May 1809], 735; Claims to Land between the Rio Hondo and Sabine Rivers, in Louisiana, January 31, 1825; *American State Papers: Public Lands*, IV, 112, 144; Sibley to William Eustis, Natchitoches, December 31, 1811, in Garrett, "Doctor John Sibley" 49 (January, 1946): 403–405.

43. Cordero to Salcedo, San Antonio, June 29, 1807, the Bexar Archives.

44. Sibley reported that the Lewis and Alexander expedition left Natchitoches during Wilkinson's stay there, "I am pretty Confident with the knowledge of the General," and that Wilkinson read to him a letter from Salcedo complaining of Sibley's "interfering with Indians who live in the Country Claimed by the King of Spain," remarking of it that the Jefferson administration "would consider that Complaint against me as the highest praise" (Sibley to Dearborn, Natchitoches, November 20, 1808, in Garrett, "Doctor John Sibley" 47 [July, 1943]: 50).

45. American documents on the Lewis and Alexander expedition are Sibley, *Report from Natchitoches*, entry for June 25, pp. 40–42; Sibley to Dearborn, Natchitoches, July 3, 1807, and November 20, 1808, in Garrett, "Doctor John Sibley" 45 (April, 1942): 381–82, and 47 (July, 1943): 50.

46. Except where otherwise noted, the source on the Grand Council in Natchitoches is Sibley, *Report from Natchitoches*, entries for August 9–18 and October 15–25, pp. 48–66, 69–76.

47. Sibley, *Report from Natchitoches*, entry for August 18, pp. 54–55. Sibley notes that his actions respecting the Comanches were being encouraged by Zebulon Pike, who had been escorted from Chihuahua through Texas by the Spaniards and had arrived in Natchitoches on June 30. Perhaps he really meant "had been encouraged," for Pike does not seem to have remained in Natchitoches long enough for the council. See Pike's entry for July 1, 1807, in Jackson, *Journals Pike*, II, 447–48, and Jackson's note; also, Sibley to Samuel Hopkins, Natchitoches, June 30, 1807, in Whittington, "Dr. John Sibley of Natchitoches," 503.

48. In fact, each Congress since American independence had passed laws prohibiting the sale of firearms and ammunition to Indians, but enforcement was impossible, and exceptions (particularly when diplomatic ties were at stake) were sometimes made. See Frank McNitt, *The Indian Traders*, 47–48, for a discussion. Although this 1807 report was submitted to the War Department, Sibley carefully avoided any further mention to Dearborn that his traders might have been trafficking in guns. Probably it was understood.

49. Sources on Andrew Glass and Anthony Glass's early years are Claiborne, *Mississippi As a Province*, 352, 534–35, nn.; Dunbar Rowland, *History of Mississippi: The Heart of the South*, II, 846; Petition to Congress by Citizens of the Territory, [August 25, 1802], *Territory of Mississippi*, V, 171; May Wilson McBee, ed. and trans., Natchez Court Records, 1767–1805, which feature many Glass entries in the land-claims volumes; interview with Mrs. Ceress Newell, Spartanburg, South Carolina, December 12, 1982. I am indebted to Mrs. Newell, a descendant of Anthony Glass, for sharing her genealogical information on him and on the Glass-Hyland families of Mississippi.

50. The story originally appeared in Otto A. Rothert's *The Outlaws of Cave-in-Rock*, based upon Rothert's license with court testimony against Samuel Mason, January 11, 1803, at New Madrid (manuscript of the proceedings in the Mississippi Department of Archives and History, Jackson). Rothert inferred from the testimony of two witnesses—who mentioned that Glass (or "Gass") had been robbed on the Natchez Trace the same day that a Kentuckian named Campbell was murdered there and that he "had been a poor man" before befriending Revolutionary War veteran Mason upon the latter's

arrival at Natchez in 1802—that Glass was a "fence" for Mason's stolen goods. No charges or real accusations were brought against Glass in this affair, but subsequent works have elaborated and embellished Rothert's version of the story. Jonathan Daniels, in his popular account *The Devil's Backbone: The Story of the Natchez Trace*, 102–104, 110–13, 120–21, for example, portrays Glass as "gleaming with pretensions of respectability" while at the same time supposedly marking the trace "with his crimes" and helping "to rob and bleed it."

51. Sibley to Dearborn, Natchitoches, November 20, 1808, in Garrett, "Doctor John Sibley" 47 (July, 1943): 50. Sibley says that Glass executed the usual bond with security of $1,000. The Natchez Court Records for the period 1797–1805, Land Claims (especially Book B) and Unrecorded Land Claims (in Hendricks, Mississippi Court Records) prove that the Glass expedition was far from being an organized, general movement of men against Spanish possessions. Rather, the party was composed essentially of Mississippi settlers who owned adjoining farms near the Big Black River, who had worked with one another on small land claims for years and who shared information, no doubt, on the life thriving contemporaneously on the Great Plains to the west. On Glass's request to settle in Texas and the negative Spanish reaction, see Glass to Cordero, Nacogdoches, October 21, 1807, and N. Salcedo to Viana, Chihuahua, January 2, 1808, Bexar Archives.

52. John Carr to Claiborne, Natchitoches, July 14, 1808. Quoted in Claiborne to Secretary of State Madison, Opelousas, August 8, 1808 (the originals of the Carr letters have been lost), Carter and Bloom, *Territorial Papers*, IX, 798–800. Also, Herrera to Cordero, San Antonio, August 14, 1808, enclosing a copy of Juan Cortes's letter, the Bexar Archives. "Clouds of Americans" would follow Glass, Cortes warned in his missive, if the project were successful. His solution: "I wish you could catch and hang them all." Like that of so many borderers, Cortes's loyalty had commodity value. Despite his informant role (in 1806 he had similarly worked against the Freeman and Custis expedition), Salcedo passed him over in favor of Marcel Soto when both wanted the Bayou Pierre agency that summer. See Salcedo to Cordero, Chihuahua, June 14 and August 26, 1808, the Bexar Archives. By 1810, then, Cortes became an employee of the Americans, working as Linnard's assistant in Natchitoches (Linnard, ledger entry for March 31, 1810, Natchitoches–Sulphur Fork Agency Ledgers, 1809–21, National Archives Record Group T1029, Washington, D.C.).

53. Claiborne to Madison, Opelousas, August 8, 1808, *Territorial Papers*, IX, 800.

54. Carr to Claiborne, Natchitoches, July 12, 1808. Quoted in *Territorial Papers*, IX. Also, Claiborne to Carr, County of Attakapas, August 8, 1808; Claiborne to Sibley, Attakapas, August 9, 1808; Claiborne to Madison, New Orleans, August 31, 1808, all in Rowland, *Official Letter-Books*, IV, 187–200.

55. In addition to the above letters, also Claiborne to Colonel Thompson, Attakapas, August 11, 1808 (Rowland, *Official Letter-Books*, IV, 190), in which Claiborne most strongly postulates a relationship between Glass and the recent Burr Conspiracy, arguing that among "the many unprincipled adventurers . . . there are no doubt some, who may yet be disposed to engage in Schemes hostile to the peace of Society."

56. Sibley to Dearborn, Natchitoches, November 20, 1808, in Garrett, "Doctor John Sibley," 47 (July, 1943): 49–51. This entire letter is devoted to a defense of the Glass expedition and begins: "The Object of this letter is to explain to you a Circumstance which I have reason to believe has been falsely represented & from evil Intentions."

57. Glass was *not* a commissioned officer of any rank and does not appear either in

Francis B. Heitman, *Historical Register and Dictionary of the United States Army*, or in William H. Powell, *List of Officers of the Army of the United States from 1779 to 1900*.

58. The quote above is from Amangual's journal, which preserves the text of a speech he repeated to several Comanche bands, entry for April 25, 1808. The journal appears in Loomis and Nasatir, *Pedro Vial*, as "Diary of Francisco Amangual from San Antonio to Santa Fe, March 30–May [June] 19, 1808," assembled from the two fragmentary versions extant. Amangual was a 69-year-old veteran who had once looked for Philip Nolan. His orders for the expedition were sent by N. Salcedo to Cordero on January 12, 1808. On Marcel Soto's expedition, see N. Salcedo to Cordero, Chihuahua, April 19 and August 26, 1808. Cordero quickly relayed news of the Glass expedition to Salcedo, but both men agreed that a force should not be sent after him lest it disturb the precarious peace. Salcedo ordered all such plans (originating with Viana in Nacogdoches) cancelled (Salcedo to Cordero, Chihuahua, August 26, 1808). All of these letters in the Bexar Archives.

59. A check of Sibley's papers preserved in Natchitoches and in the Sibley Letter-Books in the Missouri Historical Society, Saint Louis, has failed to turn up Glass's list of trade goods. Six firms in Natchitoches during the period—those of Compere and Hertzog, Vienne and Landray, Paire and Tauzin, Duval and Lauve and establishments run by A. Sampayrae and Juan Cortes—stocked goods for the Indian trade and may have been sources for the contents of their packs (see the memorial of Natchitoches Merchants to Governor Claiborne, Natchitoches, January 4, 1812, in Carter and Bloom, *Territorial Papers*, IX, 976–78).

60. See Linnard, ledger entry for February 6, 1811, Natchitoches–Sulphur Fork Agency Ledgers, 1809–1821, which includes a year's list of wanted trade goods covering some three manuscript pages. Eugene C. Barker's Francis Smith letter, published as "A Glimpse of the Texas Fur Trade in 1832," *Southwestern Historical Quarterly* 32 (1928): 279–82, is useful for the same end at a later period. According to Linnard in 1811, insofar as firearms were concerned, the Red River tribes had very specific ideas: they wanted rifles with barrels at least four feet long, carrying 60 to 70 balls to the pound (about .35 caliber). That year Linnard requested thirty such woodland Pennsylvania-Kentucky rifles for the Natchitoches trade, along with 4,000 flints and 2,000 pounds of DuPont F, FX, and E black powder.

Part 2. The Journal

1. Natchitoches to the Taovaya-Wichita Villages, June–August, 1808

1. Glass actually mentions only ten. The eleventh is Joseph Lucas, the métis interpreter, who will become one of the only expedition members to remain with Glass throughout the voyage. Seven of the party have not yet been identified in this study. Among the Natchez contingent were Ezra McCall, Joseph White, and James Davis, all of squatter families who lived near Glass in Mississippi Territory and all of whom had signed the squatters' petition circulated in the Natchez area in 1802. George Schamp and Stephen Holmes were from Natchitoches, where Holmes was homesteading (or soon would be) a farm of 660 arpens of land on the Red River, in Natchitoches Parish. Schamp and his wife, Pelagie Schamp, will in 1825 claim 5,760 acres of land on Bayou Pierre; in 1809 he will lead the Natchitoches party, which returns to purchase the meteorite from the Indians (see the Epilogue). Peter Young was from Opelousas, where he and his father had settled (La Cass Island) in 1798. At the time of this expedition he was only fifteen

years old and probably was in charge of the remuda. I have been unable to identify Jacob Low. The documents are Petition to Congress by Citizens of the Territory, [August 25, 1802], *Territorial Papers*, V, 169, 166, 164; Land Claims in the Western District of Louisiana, April 8, 1816, *American State Papers: Public Lands*, III, 199, 201; Claims to Land between the Rio Hondo and Sabine Rivers, in Louisiana, January 31, 1825, *American State Papers: Public Lands*, IV, 109.

2. Note that because they returned a wilderness commodity—live mustangs—that could not be floated on barges downriver, on this frontier trader transportation most typically was overland, by packhorse.

Located at the intersection of several important wilderness roads, the Salt Works was a logical rendezvous for the contingents from the two towns. Moreover, in 1808 it was owned by Sibley, who was engaged in the manufacture of salt. This was an old and well-known location in Louisiana; Father Pichardo believed they were the same salines found by DeSoto's army in 1540. See Charles Wilson Hackett, ed. and trans., *Pichardo's Treatise on the Limits of Louisiana and Texas*, II, 58. The starting point for the Glass expedition is thus near the modern town of Goldonna, Township 12 N., Range 5 W., Natchitoches Parish. U.S.G.S. Survey, Shreveport Quadrangle, scale 1:250,000, indicates that they would have to have traveled about fifteen miles to reach Black Lake and Brushy ("Caney") Creek, their first camp. My thanks to Carol Wells, archivist at the Watson Memorial Library at Northwestern State University, Natchitoches, for her help in untangling the local historical geography.

3. William Darby's 1816 "Map of Louisiana" calls this road the "Quechata Path or Wilderness Road." Their camp is on Grand Bayou, just north of Hall Summit, Red River Parish.

4. Into Bienville Parish to west of Ringgold, where they camp on Loggy Bayou. The native whitetail deer of this area, *Dama macroura virginiana*, is now extirpated and has been replaced with stocked animals from other states.

5. "Tulin" was François Grappe, a métis hunter raised at La Harpe's Post in the great Kadohadacho village above the Great Bend of Red River. He was Sibley's principal informant on Indians of the area and had guided the Freeman and Custis expedition. His vacherie (stock ranch), purchased from a Caddo Indian in 1787, was in Township 16 N., Range 10 W. (Bienville Parish), and was a well-known landmark on the eastern shore of Lake Bisteneau (Sibley, "Historical Sketches," 54; *Biographical and Historical Memoirs of Northwest Louisiana*, 296).

The Glass party appears to camp this night on Cooley Creek, across the lake from modern Bisteneau State Park.

6. Detouring around Lake Bisteneau and the Great Raft swamplands on the east side, they are in the longleaf-pine highlands south of present Minden, Webster Parish.

7. The "large creek" is Bayou Dorcheat, which they cross somewhere west of Minden. The tree growth he refers to is the sugar hackberry, *Celtis laevigata*.

8. Into present Bossier Parish, to a camp at Bellevue Prairie. Glass uses the French term, *prairie*, to describe a grassy opening, but it is unfamiliar enough to cause him (or the copyist) some problem with spelling.

9. Bayou Bodcau, which they cross about two miles west of Bellevue.

10. They are on Cypress Bayou, east of present Benton, Bossier Parish.

11. They have camped just behind Ollie Holm Lake and Cedar Bluffs, the river location (fixed by Thomas Freeman at 32°47' two years earlier) of the Alabama-Coushatta village since these Indians' arrival in the Caddo country in 1804. The Alabama-Coushattas were Upper Creeks who had formerly resided in present Mississippi and Ala-

bama but had retreated westward as the Americans had approached their towns. Several log-cabin villages of them dotted the streams of southeast Texas. Jean Louis Berlandier said of them: "The Conchates do not look like a native people. To see them you would say they were a gathering of settlers" (Berlandier, *The Indians of Texas in 1830*, 124). For a history of this village, occupied from 1804 to about 1835, see Dan Flores, "The Red River Branch of the Alabama-Coushatta Indians: An Ethnohistory," *Southern Studies Journal* 16 (Spring, 1977): 55–72.

12. Glass's reference to an earlier Caddo occupation of this area perhaps refers to Yatasi Caddo settlements of the eighteenth century (see the excellent map in John R. Swanton's *Source Material on the History and Ethnology of the Caddo Indians*, 8-A), which were early wiped out by disease epidemics. But perhaps the reference is to a brief occupation of Caddo Prairie, mentioned in Sibley's "Historic Sketches," 1076, as dating from 1791, the site of which Glass seems to pass on July 17. Since 1794 the Caddos under Chief Dehahuit, retreating from periodic massacres by the Osages, have abandoned all of their river villages in favor of a location on modern Jeems Bayou, a village they call Sha'-childni'ni ("Timber Hill"). When Glass says the Caddos are "on the lake," he is probably referring to Lake T'soto (Soda Lake) in the Red River bottoms. But this could be a bracketing document for the formation of Caddo Lake, in the hills to the west, by the advancing Great Raft. We know that it formed sometime during the first decade of the nineteenth century, when the Raft finally dammed Twelve-Mile Bayou. Peter Custis, describing the Caddo location in 1806, asserted that the waterway they lived on was then "a small creek." For a discussion, see Flores, *Jefferson and Southwestern Exploration*, 168–69 and n. 11.

13. In 1808 the chief of this village was named Echean. Sibley says he was "quiet & Sensible" (*Report from Natchitoches*, entries for September 7, November 10, 1807, pp. 68, 82–84), and he had personally assisted the Freeman and Custis expedition in their detour through the Great Swamp. The American flag had been given to Echean in exchange for a Spanish one the village was flying in June, 1806, during the exploring expedition's two-week layover in this village.

14. The party clearly does not stay on the northeast side of the Red River, as Sibley had promised Dearborn, but crosses it here at the Alabama-Coushatta village. They camp this evening in Caddo Prairie, probably on the site of modern Gilliam, Caddo Parish. The species of native cane so prevalent here was *Arundinaria gigantea*, a grass species introduced to science as a consequence of Jefferson's exploring surveys of the area.

15. In March of the previous year the Alabama-Coushattas had enlisted in the Caddo war with the Osages when a small hunting party of them had discovered twenty Osage warriors hunting bison in the Blackland Prairie. These Osages had recently stolen seventy Caddo horses. Waiting until nightfall, the Alabama-Coushattas had attacked, killing five of the dreaded Osages and routing the party. Forty of the stolen horses had been recaptured, a large number of which were returned to the Caddos (Sibley, *Report from Natchitoches*, entry for March 20, 1807, pp. 15–16).

16. Following Caddo Prairie, they cross present Louisiana Highway 2 and camp somewhere east of Mira. The existence of peach trees (*Prunus persica*), a tree early introduced into North America by Europeans and widely transplanted by the Indians, indicates that the remnant lodges were historic. Their frames constructed with durable red cedar poles, the ruins of Caddo lodges often took decades to crumble. Numerous mounds and sites still exist in this area today. The best overview of Caddo Prairie archaeology is Clarence Webb, *The Belcher Mound: A Stratified Caddoan Site in Caddo Parish, Louisiana*.

17. No mileage figure is given; evidently they pass out of Louisiana through the hilly terrain northeast of Rodessa, probably through the corner of Miller County, Arkansas, to a camp somewhere in southeastern Cass County, Texas.

18. Glass's route must now be followed on U.S.G.S. Texarkana Quadrangle, scale 1:250,000. They pass east of present Atlanta, and appear to camp north of Queen City.

19. The "dividing ridge" lies between the Sulphur River and the northern tributaries of Black Bayou; in this stretch the divide is only two or three miles south of the Sulphur River, occasionally providing overlooks of the prairie along it. They here travel through the rough, iron-ore pine lands near present Atlanta State Park. Benny Cash and I hiked this area in January, 1983, cutting across the trail the Glass party must have followed along the high ridge back just south of the river valley, and noticed that the least rainfall made the rapid creeks run rusty.

20. The route of the Indian trace from the Alabama-Coushattas to the Taovayas here parallels Texas Highway 77 between Douglassville and Naples. At this point they are still traversing the great virgin East Texas forest, dominated by lofty loblolly and shortleaf pines (see Robert A. Vines, *Trees of East Texas*, xiv–xv). Glass's mention of Caddo hunting paths here, and later, supports the idea that the Caddos intensively hunted across northeast Texas and the Blackland Prairie, with—he seems to say—some noticeable ecological effects. The Alabama-Coushattas had been hunting wildlife for the market since their arrival on the Red River; Sibley remarked in 1805 that one family of them had taken 118 black bears, while a single hunter had killed 400 deer in 1804 and had sold the hides for 50 cents each (Sibley, "Historical Sketches," 1079–80).

21. Along or near Highway 77 to a campsite northwest of the Cusseta Mountains, Cass County.

22. Francisco Viana's route is indicated on Fray José María de Jesús Puelles's *Mapa Geographica de las Provincias Septentrionales de esta Nueva España* (1807), in the Map Collection of the Barker Texas History Center, University of Texas at Austin. It is interesting that visible sign of the passage of the Spanish army through these woodlands still lingers two years later (Glass has the year wrong).

Glass's party has now entered the Post-Oak Savannah, for which Glass provides this terse but important early description; with the suppression of natural and Indian fires it has since become overgrown and lost much of the parkland effect suggested here. The "handsome Prararies" he describes were dominated by little bluestem (*Schizachyrium scoparium* var. *frequens*), a beautiful, knee-high bunchgrass that served as climax vegetation over most of the prairie country he will traverse. Climax tree growth of the Post-Oak Savannah was sand post oak (*Quercus margaretta*) and blackjack oak (*Q. marilandica*) along with the hickories (*Carya* spp.) and ashes (*Fraxinus* spp.) he mentions (Frank Gould, *The Grasses of Texas*, 3; Vines, *Trees of East Texas*, 47, 86, 110, 469–73). Glass's favorable impression of the prairies he sees here seems to bear out Terry Jordan's thesis that Anglo pioneers, far from avoiding these prairies, preferred them for pioneer farms (Terry Jordan, "Pioneer Evaluation of Vegetation in Frontier Texas," *Southwestern Historical Quarterly* 76 (1973): 233–54).

23. Probably to northwest of Naples, into Morris County.

24. They cross White Oak Creek just south of present Interstate 30. The lake Glass proceeds to describe is a natural lake that remains today; it can be viewed north of I-30 about two miles east of the White Oak Creek bridge.

25. Continuing along the Sulphur River (still south of the main branch) in an undulating prairie, which takes them near to present Talco and the Franklin County

line. This is the most easterly of the large natural prairies of northeast Texas, and the country rapidly is changing, as appears in some subtle observations he makes here. The mounds of Sulphur Prairie still startle the traveler passing through this country, the rolling pasturelands giving the appearance of being fairly pimpled with them. Geologists, who grappled with their origins for decades, now believe that the sandy materials of which they are composed were laid down in late Wisconsin time, and that the mounds represent "residual soil hillocks" let down to bedrock by subsequent erosion of intervening material. These natural mounds occur widely in the near Southwest and spottily near the Central Rockies (Carl C. Branson, "Patterns of Oklahoma Prairie Mounds," *Oklahoma Geology Notes,* 26 [1966]: 263–73; F. A. Melton, "'Natural Mounds' of Northeast Texas, Southern Arkansas, and Northern Louisiana," *Oklahoma Academy of Sciences, Proceedings* 9 [1929]: 119–30).

Glass also has this day his first encounter with a true prairie species: greater prairie chickens (*Tympanuchus cuprido americanus*), a plump grouse of the humid, tall-grass prairies. As late as 1850 there still were half a million of these birds in the North Texas prairies, but market hunting and habitat alteration by agriculture extirpated them completely. No attempt was made to save them; the last flocks were seen near Marshall in 1920 (Harry C. Oberholser, *The Bird Life of Texas* I, 265–67; Robin Doughty, *Wildlife and Man in Texas,* 61).

26. They cross the main branch of the Sulphur River somewhere in the vicinity of Mobberly and camp west of Bogota, in Red River County. Glass's party is now on the edge of the Blackland Prairie, which stretches in a long strip from the Balcones Escarpment northward 400 miles to the Ouachita Mountains. In its natural state it was a rolling bluestem prairie, with swell crests about a mile apart, and many thickly timbered creeks that cut deep channels in the waxey black soil. Their party has thus reached the beginning of the "Great Plains," as contemporaries called them, and encounters with mustangs, bison, and other "Western" novelties will increase. According to the June, 1984, newsletter of the Native Prairies Association of Texas, less than one-half of one percent of the Blackland is left in original prairie condition today.

27. The only plum in this range that fits the description is the Chickasaw plum (*Prunus angustifolia*), a thicket-forming shrub of five to fifteen feet, found principally at the edges of prairies. The Chickasaw plum probably was native here, but it was widely transplanted by Indians farther east because of its excellent fruit (Robert Vines, *The Trees of North Texas,* 226–28). The "Beautiful Creeks" they cross today are Mustang, Brushy, Bee, Little Sandy, and Big Sandy.

28. This is a surprising entry, for what natural history particulars Glass gives on these "Prararie Squirrels" do not sound right for the thirteen-lined ground squirrel (*Citellus tridecemlineatus*), today found in the Blackland, but seem instead to fit the black-tailed prairie dog (*Cyonomys ludovicianus ludovicianus*). Based largely upon Vernon Bailey's zoological survey of 1905, the eastward range of this species in Texas has long been fixed at about 98° W. There has been some archaeological work, however, indicating that this prairie dog did once range farther east. Blackland clays would have supported their tunnels, and divides where bison and mustangs trampled the grass down would have been good habitat. Glass therefore may provide us with a rare documentation for the existence of relict prairie-dog colonies on the Blackland Prairie of the early nineteenth century. See E. Raymond Hall and Keith R. Kelson, *The Mammals of North America,* I, 245–47; Bob H. Slaughter and Ronald Ritchie, "Pleistocene Mammals of the Clear Creek Local Fauna, Denton County, Texas," *Journal of the [SMU] Graduate Re-*

search Center 31 (1963), 117–31; B. H. Slaughter and W. L. McClure, "The Sims Bayou Local Fauna: Pleistocene of Houston, Texas," *Texas Academy of Science Journal* 17 (1965): 404–17.

29. Glass helps us fix the original range of the Osage orange (*Maclura pomifera*), a tree whose appearance farther east seems now to have been the result of Indian transplanting. It is a narrow endemic, the center of its range lying arthwart the Red River and extending 200 miles both north and south, and westward from the Blackland to the Western Cross Timbers. The bois d'arc had been described to Jefferson by both Sibley and Meriwether Lewis in 1804, but the first published details of it, with the assertion that it was a genus new to science, was by Peter Custis in 1806 (see Dan Flores, "The Ecology of the Red River in 1806: Peter Custis and Early Southwestern Natural History," *Southwestern Historical Quarterly* 88 (July, 1984): 33. They have crossed the prairie to near Honey Grove and the Fannin County line. The two creeks seem to be Hickory Creek (or the Chick branch of it) and Auds Creek, due south of Paris in Lamar County.

30. They are now between Honey Grove and Bonham, and can be traced on U.S.G.S. Sherman Quadrangle, scale 1:250,000.

31. The crossing of Bois d'Arc Creek, a favorite beaver stream of the old French hunters, seems to be effected near Bonham. This first mention of "great numbers" of bison and mustangs seems to refer to the country between Bonham and the Grayson County line. In his "Prehistoric Bison Populations of Northcentral Texas," *Bulletin of the Texas Archeological Society* 50 (1980): 89–101, Mark Lynott uses archaeological evidence to argue that bison populations were never large in the Prairie–Cross Timbers country, primarily because the nutritional value of bluestem was less suited to bison needs than the shorter grasses farther west, and that whitetail deer were always the more important subsistence animal in the area (see, however, Glass's comment in Section 2). Ecologists, who argue that modern bison were a "weed" species that steadily filled niches vacated by the extinction of two dozen American grazers/browsers during the late Pleistocene, believe that bison were expanding their range eastward about the time Euroamericans arrived in the New World (see some of the arguments of papers appearing in Paul S. Martin and Henry E. Wright, Jr., eds., *Pleistocene Extinctions: The Search for a Cause*). By Glass's time a contraction was operating in the face of Indian and white hunting pressure. According to Jerry N. McDonald's *North American Bison: Their Classification and Evolution*, 263, this southern Great Plains bison phenotype was probably hunted to complete extinction.

32. Crossing a tributary of Choctaw Creek, the party passes between present Sherman and Denison. The "old camp" which Alexander and Lucas had made on the 1806–1807 expedition was probably in the vicinity of present Hagerman National Wildlife Refuge.

33. Depending upon their exact route, at some point during the last two days they have crossed the Eastern Cross Timbers, a thick strip of oak woods, which must have slowed their progress considerably. They seem to ford the river somewhere between present Gainesville and Marietta, Oklahoma. Once again on the prairies, they spot across the slight roll of present Love County what must have been to these early traders the "pilot knobs" for this stretch of the trail, which in this flat country give the illusion of being much higher than they are. The loftiest of them was today's Peak Hill, which rises to a height of only about 165 feet above the surrounding country. One of the others probably was Flattop Peak. Glass's "knobbs" can be seen today by travelers driving north on I-35 from the Red River crossing, about two miles east of Marietta. See U.S.G.S. Marietta East Quadrangle, scale 7.5'.

34. They are in the Grand Prairie, a strip of beautifully rolling plain (actually remnant Cretaceous ocean terraces) lying between the Eastern and Western Cross Timbers. Originally clothed with little bluestem, big bluestem (*Andropogon gerardii*), switchgrass (*Panicum virgatum*), and diangrass (*Sorghastrum nutans*), the Grand Prairie was bison range *par excellence*. Farther south it had been Philip Nolan's favorite mustanging country. For the native vegetation, see Gould, *Grasses of Texas*, 2–3.

35. The Western Cross Timbers. Josiah Gregg, the Santa Fe trader, described these once well-known landmarks thus: "The Cross Timbers vary in width from five to thirty miles, and entirely cut off the communication betwixt the interior prairies and those of the great plains. They may be considered as the 'fringe' of the great prairies, being a continuous brushy strip, composed of various kinds of undergrowth; such as blackjacks, post-oaks, and in some places hickory, elm, etc., intermixed with a very diminutive dwarf oak, called by the hunters, 'shin-oak.' Most of the timber appears to be kept small by the continual inroads of the 'burning prairies;' for being killed almost annually, it is constantly replaced by scions of undergrowth; so that it becomes more and more dense every reproduction" (Josiah Gregg, *Commerce of the Prairies*, II, 200).

36. Five weeks after leaving Natchitoches, the Glass party has arrived at the principal Taovayas village. Founded around 1757, apparently with encouragement of French traders, this village was situated on the northeast bank of the Red River in what is now Jefferson County, Oklahoma, at the intersection of 33°59′N. and 97°36′W. The location, at the juncture of the Western Cross Timbers with the Great Plains, was an environmentally rich one, enabling these agricultural and hunting people to enjoy a high living standard. Francisco Fragoso, who traveled widely in the early Southwest and visited the Taovayas location in 1788, concluded that "the harmony [among them] is great, since the country is the most beautiful that I have seen" (Francisco Fragoso, "Diary, Santa Fe to Natchitoches, June 24, 1788–August 20, 1789," entry for July 20, 1788, in Loomis and Nasatir, *Pedro Vial*, 339). The location was also a strategic one, at the edge of the Comanchería and at the head of navigation on the Red, both greatly contributing to the success of the location as a trade center. For half a century before Glass, French traders had been floating barges of wilderness products—and often Apache slaves—down the river from these villages.

Over the years, with frequent migrations of Wichitas, Skidis, Iscanis, Kichais, Tawakonis, and Taovayas into and from this village and the two across the river, its size had fluctuated. In 1808 it probably contained thirty to forty lodges. The Americans followed the French in referring to this village as a Taovayas town, but the reality may have been a mix of bands, including Skidis, Iscanis (Wacos), and perhaps Kichais, in addition to Taovayas. In fact, the journal's name for this village, "Quich," is probably a phonetic struggle with the word Kichai. In 1830 Berlandier referred to the Kichais as the "Quichas" (*The Indians of Texas in 1830*, 141). As the fortified site of the famous Parilla battle of 1759 and "the most important archaeological site in Oklahoma," this village was the object of much scientific attention in the 1960s. See Tyler Bastian, "Initial Report on the Longest Site," *Great Plains Newsletter* 3 (1966): 1–3; and Robert E. Bell and Tyler Bastian, "Preliminary Report upon Excavations at the Longest Site, Oklahoma," in Robert E. Bell, Edward B. Jelks, and W. W. Newcomb, *A Pilot Study Of Wichita Indian Archeology and Ethnohistory*, 54–118. The most capable historical study of the Taovayas is the one done by Elizabeth A. Harper John: "The Taovayas Indians in Frontier Trade and Diplomacy, 1719–1835," in three parts: 1, *The Chronicles of Oklahoma* 31 (1952); 2, *Southwestern Historical Quarterly* 57 (1952): 181–201; 3, *Panhandle-Plains Historical Review* 46 (1953): 41–72.

37. The American flag already flying in the Taovayas village is one Lewis and Alexander had brought the year before. Glass does not tell us exactly when he presents the Indians the flag he has been traveling under, but it will go to the Wichita village across the river.

During the week of Glass's arrival among the Indians, passionate letters regarding his expedition are emanating from Governor Claiborne and from General Herrera in San Antonio (see the introduction).

2. Life among the Indians, August–October, 1808

1. Glass renders his name later in the journal "Awahakea." Sibley's spelling of the name, Awahakei, is the form that has entered the literature. Sibley tells us that the name meant "Great Bear" and describes him as "the Great Tawiache Chief the first Man in the Nation, who every body Speaks well of." Awahakei was, in fact, the central personality in the Taovaya-Wichita complex of villages on the Red River, and the presence now of American traders in them seems to have been as much a consequence of his activity as of Sibley's. In October of 1807 he had personally visited Natchitoches to seek closer ties with the Americans, for which he had received from Sibley a U.S. medal, an officer's uniform coat, and "One Handsome Welted Philadelphia made Saddle." Awahakei had treated the Lewis and Alexander party with great deference and had "invited" the Glass expedition to "a trading fare"—one that, incidentally, does not materialize (Sibley, "Historical Sketches," 1081; Sibley, *Report from Natchitoches*, entry for June 25, 1807, pp. 40–41, entry for October 18, 1807, p. 71; Sibley to Eustis, Natchitoches, December 31, 1811, in Garrett, "Doctor John Sibley," 49 [January, 1946]: 413).

2. In the manuscript Sibley has crossed out the copyist's carefully transcribed "women" and substituted "warriors." But judging from other, corroborating, accounts of the participation of women in Caddoan councils—as well as further examples from Glass—"women" does indeed seem the word intended. See, for example, de Mézières's account of 1778, in Bolton, *Athanase de Mézières*, II, 203: "Their government is democratic, not even excluding the women, in consideration of what they contribute to the welfare of the republic." What, in fact, set Caddoan women apart was the economic importance of the female-managed Caddoan gardens and a history of women village leaders in Caddoan tradition. In addition, Taovaya-Wichita society was strongly matriarchal and matrilocal in residence.

3. The Neutral Ground agreement of 1806, of course, had relieved the two governments of the immediate necessity of a settlement. As previously mentioned, that agreement had left unresolved the status of Taovaya, Wichita, Tawakoni, and Comanche lands on the upper Red River. The final drawing of the boundary in the Adams-Onís treaty of 1819 was based upon hydrography rather than tribal claims. Use of the Red River as the international boundary effectively cleaved the various groups between the United States and Spain, or later Mexico.

4. In their watershed study *The Comanches: Lords of the South Plains*, Ernest Wallace and E. Adamson Hoebel write that the "Early French explorers and the few Americans who penetrated the Great Plains" knew the Comanches as "Padoucas" (p. 4). But this is obviously not correct, for all of the Americans of this period—Sibley, Wilkinson, Pike, Dearborn, and now Glass—call the Comanches "Hietans" or "Ietans." According to Jackson, *Journals of Pike*, I, 190 n. 3, the term was a Siouan word "picked up by early traders." It seems to have been applied to all the mountain-based Shoshonean speakers, including the Utes and Shoshones. Father Pichardo, Sibley's Texas

critic, believed the Natchitoches Indian agent was responsible for the widespread use of "Hietan" in reference to the Comanches but insisted that Sibley misapplied the word and that "Hietan" should have been reserved for the Utes only. I strongly suspect that the word entered Sibley's frontier circle from traders Nolan, Ashley, and House. See Sibley, "Historical Sketches," 1082; and Hackett, *Pichardo's Treatise*, II, 255.

5. The phonetic rendering of this phrase may be incomplete or imprecise, but it appears to carry the meaning: "You have my strong words" (a:=possessive; wakhaʔi= speak; keʔes=you will; kas=intensifier). See the Wichita-English Morpheme Index in David S. Rood, *A Wichita Grammar*, 277–92.

6. Glass indentifies a complex of cultivars whose varieties we can only guess at today. The corn-beans-squash complex was typical of Amerindian agriculturalists in North America, but the fact that these Indians grew profuse harvests of the introduced Asiatic muskmelon (*Cucumis melo*) and African watermelons (*Citrullus vulgaris*) is indicative of the influence of the early French traders on their culture. Glass tells us more about the size of their fields than any other chronicler. From these plots they grew enough surplus food to use for exchange as a trade commodity. In typical Caddoan fashion, their fields seem to have been in the river floodplain, and consequently they were not plagued by declining fertility.

7. Glass does not offer much about the Taovaya-Wichita "grass houses" not mentioned by other observers. The lodges of their permanent villages were classically southern Caddoan (as distinct from the earthen lodges of the Nebraska Pawnees): beehive-shaped structures made of cedar saplings, willow switches, and grass matting. Religious symbolism was a feature of this architecture, with east-west doorways permitting the observation of sunrise and sunset, support poles arranged in the cardinal directions to divide the dwelling into the four world quarters, and celestial, clan, or totem figures painted on the outside. Further details of house construction and attendant ceremony may be found in George A. Dorsey, *The Mythology of the Wichita*, 4–5. See, also, Waldo Wedel, "Native Astronomy and the Plains Caddoans," in Anthony F. Aveni, ed., *Native American Astronomy*, 138–39.

8. The Taovayas chief has provided us with some interesting particulars on the migrations of his people and the reasons for them. It is now believed, using the linguistic method called glottochronology, that the Plains Caddoan groups separated from the Caddoan speakers of the Red River valley some 3,000 years ago, and that Pawnee-Wichita divergence took place about 1,000–1,500 years after (around the time of the early Christian era in Rome). Increasingly, archaeologists are suggesting that the Wichitan peoples may once have occupied Texas Panhandle sites (the Antelope Creek culture along the Canadian) before moving northeast to the Great Bend of the Arkansas, where Coronado met them as "Quiverans" in 1541. The Pawnees, including the Skidis, were meanwhile settled on the Platte River and its tributaries. No scholar believes that Wichitan peoples ever settled north of the Smokey Hill River. See the recent series of articles in *Nebraska History* 60 (1979), especially Waldo Wedel, "Some Reflections on Plains Caddoan Origins," 273, 277; Douglas R. Parks, "The Northern Caddoan Languages: Their Subgrouping and Time Depths," 205–207; Christopher Lintz, "The Southwestern Periphery of the Plains Caddoan Area," 161–81; and, also, Jack Thomas Hughes, "Prehistory of the Caddoan-Speaking Tribes," in *Caddoan Indians III*, 320–21.

A series of European observers (Oñate in 1601; La Harpe in 1719; de la Bruyére in 1741) provide corroboration for a gradual dispersal of Wichitan bands southward to the Canadian and by 1736 to near the Kadohadachos on the Red. Following their 1747 alliance with the Comanches (which may or may not have been effected with the assistance of French traders), the historic villages of the eighteenth and nineteenth centuries were founded on the middle Brazos and by 1757 on the Red River. See, for ease in tracing these migrations, W. W. Newcomb and W. T. Field's "A Calendrical Summary of Wichita Ethnohistory," in Bell et al., *Wichita Indian Archeology*, 243–71.

Awahakei may be a bit older than Glass believes, but his testimony is important, indicating that there were still Taovayas settlements on the Arkansas as late as 1750.

9. From the time of La Harpe's explorations of the Southwest in 1719, the Tawakonis had appeared in the documents in close association with the Taovayas, Wichitas, and Iscanis. They appear to have been the vanguard in the migration to the south. Father Calahorra, a Spanish Franciscan from the Nacogdoches mission, found a Tawakoni village on the Sabine in 1760, visiting it three times with Hasinai Caddo assistance. Antonio Treviño, the Nacogdoches soldier captured and held prisoner by the Taovayas in 1760, reported that at that time the "Tehuacanas" were fifty leagues south of the Red River villages. In 1772 de Mézières found a "Tuacana" village on the Trinity River (near present Palestine) and one on the Brazos; by 1778, however, both Tawakoni villages were on the Brazos, the larger in the vicinity of present Waco. A year after Glass's prairie tour, in the fall of 1809, Captain José de Goseascochea will visit it and call it the "Village of the Drum"; from other sources it seems that its principal leader during the period was Quiscat. Chief Concho's Tawakoni village was during the years 1808–1809 located about five miles downstream, on the opposite (west) bank. Several early explorers, including de Mézières and Pedro Vial, have left us accounts of these towns (José de Goseascochea, "Diary Written by Captain D. José de Goseascochea of the Incidents and War Operations Incurred by the 52 men . . . [between October 5 and November 21, 1809]," entry for October 17, 1809, the Bexar Archives; Pedro Vial, "Diary of Pedro Vial, Bexar to Santa Fe, October 4, 1786, to May 26, 1787," entries for October 23 through December 15, in Loomis and Nasatir, *Pedro Vial*, 271–73). De Mézières's descriptions are in several letters reproduced in Bolton, *Athanase de Mézières*, I, 286–89, and II, 195–96.

10. When the Spanish commander Parilla attacked the Taovayas and their French and Comanche allies in 1759, there were no villages on the south bank. But when the Opelousas trader, J. Gaignard, visited the Red River tribes in 1774, there were at least two villages on the south side. De Mézières called the southerly settlement a single village in 1778 and noted that it contained 123 lodges; he named it San Bernardo. In 1787 Mares had found almost the same number of lodges on the south bank as Glass does in 1808–Mares says 23 and 40. Glass gives us some information about the ethnic composition of these towns. One is obviously a Wichita village, while the second is Taovayan (which he renders as a variation of the French term Tawéhash). Archaeologists know this site as "Spanish Fort," or the Upper Tucker site. It is located in Montague County, Texas, about one and one-half miles northeast of the present community of Spanish Fort. Preliminary work done here by National Science Foundation researchers in 1966 revealed numerous examples of European and some American trade ware, as well as the remains of several lodges. See J. Ned Woodall's "The Upper Tucker Site," in Bell et al., *Wichita Indian Archeology*, 3–13. Readers wishing to study the location of this village complex more closely should use U.S.G.S. Spanish Fort (Oklahoma-Texas) Quadrangle, scale 7.5'.

11. Like the Tawakonis, the Wichita band had always been mentioned in conjunction with the Taovayas whenever Europeans had encountered them. At one time, prior to the cultural disruption that followed their contacts with whites, the Prairie Caddoans probably constructed band-specific settlements, a variation of which continues into Glass's time. Despite the village pattern he documents here, other bands were also living in these villages. Still later in the century further fragmentation blurred all the previous

distinctions. The remaining place names of the area—Big and Little Wichita rivers, Wichita Falls, the Wichita Mountains—reflect the consolidation existing at the time Anglo pioneers settled this area.

Governor Cordero, who renders the name of this chief "Quachaeta," had ratified his selection as chief of the Wichitas—to fill the vacancy left by the death of Chief Iras Coques (Eriascoc)—only the month before, during the visit to San Antonio which Glass mentions (Note by Cordero, San Antonio, July 5, 1808, the Bexar Archives).

12. I have found no corroborating documents identifying this Taovaya subchief.

Sibley's spelling of Tawéhash was "Towiache," and he believed that this was "the proper Indian name" for the people the Americans called "Panis." At least one scholar, Ralph Smith, has preferred "Tawéhash" to the more widely used term. See his "The Tawéhash in French, Spanish, English, and American Imperial Affairs," *West Texas Historical Association Year Book* 28 (1952): 18–49.

According to Sibley, the names of the two towns on the south bank are "Witchata" and "Towaahach" (Sibley, "Historical Sketches," 1080).

13. The later Santa Fe trader, Josiah Gregg, remarked that in Indian trade the major difficulty was always at the outset. But once terms for the first horse or mule were set, subsequent transactions followed that formula and trading then went smoothly (Josiah Gregg, *Commerce on the Prairies*, II, 45–46). In this connection, W. B. Parker, in his *Notes Taken during the Expedition Commanded by Capt. R. B. Marcy . . .* , p. 234, mentions the shrewdness of the Indians in establishing the initial terms using their best animals. That these Indians were veteran barterers with white traders and were used to setting the terms on their home grounds is amply demonstrated by Glass's experiences. Very disappointing is his omission of the terms he finally established with his clients. Indians usually preferred a general assortment of goods in trade—a blanket, flint or powder, together with small quantities of tobacco, paint, and beads. A rifle-horse trade might involve several animals, depending upon the quality of the goods.

Glass's use of the term "Cavirllard" (horse herd) is a trader corruption of the Spanish *caballada*. A mule herd was a *mulada*.

14. The northern affluents of the Trinity drain the Western Cross Timbers, due south of the Taovaya-Wichita location. Since he says they are taking their herds thirty miles away, this grazing range was on what Glass will later refer to as the "Western Branch" of the Trinity. He says it heads in hilly country, so this Indian pony range would have been on the modern West Fork of the Trinity, near present Jacksboro.

Glass has here named *twelve* persons in his party. William C. Alexander, who had spent the previous summer among the Comanches, probably led the Americans in this contingent going out to find Comanches.

15. At some point during their generations of wandering in the middle prairies, the Plains Caddoans had encountered the Siouan speakers who entered history as the Osages. The time was so remote, says Awahakei, that even tradition did not recall it. But since then the enmity had become instinctive.

The Osages (the name is a corruption of their name for themselves: *Wa-zha-zhe*) were among the southernmost Siouans, one-time agriculturalists who had farmed the oak-prairie province between the Ozarks and the Missouri River. A large, physically impressive people, by the early nineteenth century they had become fierce raiders, whose guerilla tactics went somewhat beyond Glass's "game." Early locked into a dependence upon European goods, their economic and political systems had been reshaped by European policies and by a new value system emphasizing horses and guns, wealth and warrior prestige. Osage raids against the Red River tribes reached back into the eighteenth

century, but from the 1790s the harassment must have intensified. During that decade
an "Arkansas" band of Osages, led by Cashesegra and the young Clermont, set up a village near the Three Forks of the Arkansas; simultaneously, Auguste and Pierre Chouteau
established their famous trading post there. Parties from this band, which is said to have
attracted the most aggressive young warriors of the nation, will be regular "visitors"
while Glass is among the Taovayas. He will later relate that Osage raiders stole 1,000
horses from his hosts during his stay among them (Sibley to Eustis, Natchitoches, May
10, 1809, in Garrett, "Doctor John Sibley," 47 [January, 1944]: 323; Frederick Webb
Hodge, ed., Handbook of American Indians North of Mexico, II, 156; Willard H. Rollings,
"Prairie Hegemony: An Ethnohistorical Study of the Osage, from Early Times to 1840"
[Ph.D. dissertation, Texas Tech University, Lubbock, 1983], 126, 146–54). The most recent work on the Osages, emphasizing their relations with New Spain, is Gilbert C. Din
and Abraham Nasatir, The Imperial Osages: Spanish-Indian Diplomacy in the Mississippi Valley.

16. Information respecting the sign language of the Great Plains tribes had been
forwarded to Thomas Jefferson by William Dunbar following the latter's interviews with
Philip Nolan around 1800. But I believe this description by Glass is the earliest one we
have on plains horse signaling. Walter Prescott Webb, in his classic The Great Plains, 79,
has argued convincingly that horse signaling was an extension of sign gestures made with
hands and arms (in the context of his thesis, Webb believes that both were cultural adap-
tations to the immense spaces of the plains, where visual communication was possible at
much greater distances than sound could carry). An extensive nineteenth-century essay
on horse signaling may be found in Richard I. Dodge, The Hunting Grounds of the Great
West, pp. 368–69.

17. Here and later the tribal name "Tawenatas" (later "Tanveratas") cannot be identified with certainty. Elizabeth John and I have carried on considerable correspondence
over it. She conjectures that these "Tawenatas" were Grand Pawnees, known enemies of
the Comanches during this period, and has found a Spanish letter (Elguezábal to Salcedo,
San Antonio, November 21, 1804, Bexar Archives) that uses the term "Tahuiratas" in a
way that may imply Grand Pawnees. Another possibility is that the word is a garbled
version of tonkaweya. The Tonkawas were traditional enemies of the Southern Caddoans
and roamed across the Central Texas prairies and Cross Timbers, where Glass's party
would later fear attack from "Tanveratas" (Swanton, Indian Tribes, 326–27; W. W. Newcomb, Jr., The Indians of Texas, chap. 6; Deborah Lamont Newlin, The Tonkawa People:
A Tribal History from Earliest Times to 1893, 12, 22). For a new study of the Tonkawas,
see Thomas F. Schilz, "People of the Cross Timbers: A History of the Tonkawa Indians"
(Ph.D. diss., Texas Christian University, 1983).

18. "Purification" was a routine practice in Indian medicine, but Glass is the only
observer to mention it among these Indians. The use of warm water (commonly mixed
with juice from the yaupon, Ilex vomitoria) in an emetic mixture links Taovaya purification to the cultural practices of the woodlands, in contrast to the sweat-lodge favored by
the western tribes for that purpose. See Virgil Vogel, American Indian Medicine, 78–79.

19. While Glass's account is consistent with those of other observers of Taovaya-
Wichita marriage, like most Euroamerican observers he mistakes the gift-exchange
which marked such ceremonies as a "purchase" of the woman. W. W. Newcomb, Jr., in
The Indians of Texas, 261–62, notes that while this approach "was the socially correct
marriage procedure . . . poorer families apparently abridged the gift-giving. . . ."

20. There are some welcome details here and later respecting sexuality among the
Taovaya-Wichitas, a cultural facet about which most other chroniclers are silent. Only de

Mézières mentions it, when he noted with disapproval what he called "their incestuous and base intercourse, and other abominations" (Bolton, *Athanase de Mézières*, I, 295). In fact, sexual freedom for both men and women was consistent with the general liberality and egalitarianism of Taovaya-Wichita culture. Such generosity was distinctively Caddoan: Father Solís had found an exchange of sexual partners a regular practice among the Hasinais in 1767, for example. Euroamerican traders who participated were rewarded in the strong bonds thus established. See Margaret K. Kress, trans., "Diary of a Visit of Inspection of the Texas Missions Made by Fray Gaspar José de Solís in the Year 1767–68," *Southwestern Historical Quarterly* 35 (1931): 41–42.

21. Glass does not tell us anything more about the male role in agriculture than that they constructed fences around the fields to keep out stock and wild animals, but he gives the impression that they participated in routine gardening. This is interesting, for it is in contrast to what other observers noticed—Bolton, *Athanase de Mézières*, II, 203, for example: "The women tan, sew, and paint the skins, fence the fields, care for the corn fields, harvest the crops, cut and fetch the fire-wood, prepare the food, build the houses, and rear the children, their constant care stopping at nothing that contributes to the comfort and pleasure of their husbands. The latter devote themselves wholly to the chase and warfare." Anthropologists have always assumed that the Taovaya-Wichitas resembled most other hunting-agricultural societies in their division of labor based upon sex, women taking over tasks that could be done in conjunction with child care. Among the Caddos proper, however, we know that men participated in the gardening (see Newcomb, *Indians of Texas*, 298). Glass's comment here indicates that Taovaya-Wichitas may have been more strongly Caddoan in their division of labor than has heretofore been assumed.

22. The preserved pumpkin "mats" of these people frequently attracted the notice of visitors. De Mézières said of their "calabashes [pumpkins]" in 1778 (Bolton, *Athanase de Mézières*, II, 201) that "They preserve the latter from year to year, weaving them curiously like mats." Sibley commented on the practice in 1805: "the pumpkins they cut round in their shreads, and when it is in a state of dryness that is so tough it will not break, but bend, they plait and work it into large mats, in which state they sell it to the Hietans, who, as they travel, cut off and eat it as they want it" (Sibley, "Historical Sketches," 1081).

23. Archaeologists working this village site in 1966 found seven burials, all located along the bluff overlooking the river, and on the edge of the ravine near the spring where Glass first camped. See Robert E. Bell and Tyler Bastian, "Preliminary Report upon Excavations at the Longest Site, Oklahoma," in Bell et al, *Wichita Indian Archeology*, 82–84. Prior to interment, the face of the deceased would be painted with his or her personal symbols; for a warrior, the accoutrements of war would be placed in the shallow grave (see figure 40, *Wichita Indian Archeology*). Dorsey says that the period of mourning was commonly *four* days, and collected these two prayers that were recited to the Earth Mother at burials:

> We are children of the earth, and as we go on a journey it means that we are like children crawling upon our mother, and as we exist upon the earth we are kept alive by her breath, the wind, and at the end of our time we are put in the ground in the bosom of our mother.

> Now you have been made to contain all things, to produce all things, and for us to travel over. Also we have been told to take care of

everything which has come from your bosom, and we have been told that in your body everything should be buried. I now come to bury this man.

Dorsey, *Mythology of the Wichita*, 12–13, 19–20.

24. Previously it has been assumed that Taovaya-Wichita cannibalism was not practiced after about 1773, the last year it is referred to by the early visitors (W. W. Newcomb, Jr., and W. T. Field, "New Light on Wichita Culture," in Bell et al., *Wichita Indian Archeology*, 326). Glass, however, makes three clear references to cannibalism, here and in his entries for September 14 and 28. Clearly it was still being practiced in 1808. Berlandier, in fact, corroborates Glass, although the former's observation from the 1820s was not firsthand (Jean Louis Berlandier, *The Indians of Texas in 1830*, 78).

Unfortunately, his account does not clear up for us the rationale behind the practice among these Indians. We know that the parent Caddoan peoples practiced "ritualized" or "symbolic" cannibalism, in which human flesh was consumed for magical reasons to acquire the "power" or other traits of the deceased. Since Glass's remarks all pertain to cannibalism perpetrated against enemies, it is likely that here revenge was also a motive. The least satisfactory explanation is the one often advanced by early European observers, that "their favorite dish is human flesh." See Newcomb and Field, "New Light on Wichita Culture," in Bell et al., *Wichita Indian Archeology*, for a discussion.

25. "Owaheys" is a good phonetic rendering of the Indian word *Awah:i*, the Pan-Caddoan term for their relatives from the Platte, the Skidis. See Mildred M. Wedel, "The Ethnohistoric Approach to Plains Caddoan Origins," *Nebraska History* 60 (1979): 190.

What Glass is telling us here is that the historic trade connections of the Taovaya-Wichitas have traditionally been to the north and east, and hence with the English and French rather than southward with the Spanish—a fact borne out by archaeological evidence from Taovaya and Wichita village sites.

26. These cache pits, resorted to when the people abandoned their villages for the winter hunt, are also spoken of by other observers, most of whom were impressed by the industriousness of these Indians in laying back future stores. See Newcomb and Field, "New Light on Wichita Culture," in Bell et al., *Wichita Indian Archeology*, 314–15.

27. This is Glass's only reference, and a tantalizing one, to the Taovaya fortification that so confounded Parilla's attacking force of Spaniards in the Battle of Red River, 1759. Antonio Treviño, a captured Spanish soldier, is the only other eyewitness to describe this fort. He said it was built of split logs separated from one another, and was surrounded on the outside by an earthen rampart with a deep trench encircling the earthworks (statement made by Antonio Treviño, in "Procedings Concerning the Restoration of Antonio Treviño to his Presidio by the Chief of the Taguis Indians, March 20–August 26, 1765," the Bexar Archives). Since Glass appears to have seen only the earthworks, the timbers may have been used otherwise by 1808. The debate over the role of the French in the construction of this fort still divides Wichita scholars, but it ought to be noted that the fortification pattern for prairie farmers predates the founding of this village. See Waldo Wedel, "Some Aspects of Human Ecology in the Central Plains," *American Anthropologist* 55 (1953): 508.

Interestingly, photographs taken from the air of this village site in the 1960s clearly showed the outline of this fort as a large, oval-shaped ring of earth measuring about 90 by 130 yards. See Bell and Bastian, "Preliminary Report upon Excavations at the Longest Site, Oklahoma," in Bell et al., *Wichita Indian Archeology*, 59 and figure 26.

28. Glass's population figures are probably quite accurate, and are substantially in agreement with Governor Salcedo's estimate in 1809 of 400 warriors and 2,000 souls for

the Red River villages. This is, in fact, a considerable reduction from the 600 warriors and 3,000 souls de Mézières had recorded for these villages thirty years earlier. We do not have to look far for the reason, for Sibley wrote that in 1801 "a great number of them . . . were swept off by the small pox." Judging from the relative figures, then, nearly a third of the populace of these towns must have been destroyed. This recent epidemic may have seriously weakened Taovaya-Wichita cosmology and faith in the traditional healing practices, as will shortly be seen (Bolton, *Athanase de Mézières*, II, 294; Sibley, "Historical Sketches," 1082; Newcomb and Field, "An Estimation of Wichita Population," in Bell et al., *Wichita Indian Archeology*, 349–54).

29. According to Sibley's letter to Professor Benjamin Silliman, Natchitoches, June 2, 1822, The Silliman Family Collection, Historical Manuscripts Collection, Yale University, New Haven, this migration tradition was collected by him rather than Glass and inserted into the Glass manuscript by the copyist (my speculation as to why appears in the epilogue). No other chronicle, in fact, records this migration tradition, which probably was collected from a Skidi (since the point of origin is the Platte River).

As with many Indian oral traditions, the landmarks are "the reality in the haze." The Salt Plain of this tradition does exist: today it is the site of a Great Salt Plain National Wildlife Refuge and an Oklahoma State Park, headquartered at nearby Enid. For additional information see Martha Royce Blaine, "Mythology and Folklore: Their Possible Use in the Study of Plains Caddoans Origins," *Nebraska History* 60 (1979): 240–41.

30. The Nadako, also called Anadarko (the name of the Oklahoma town around which the remnant Caddoans now reside), were an affiliated tribe of the Hasinai Confederacy of the Angelina and Neches rivers. By 1808 these groups had been drastically reduced by disease, and numerous consolidations had taken place. But according to Sibley, the Nadakos still inhabited a separate village on the Sabine River, with a population of 200 souls (Sibley, "Historical Sketches," 1077–78). This Nadako will be appropriated as a messenger by Glass to carry a letter to Sibley. See section 3, 17, for the less than satisfactory outcome.

31. Glass's description here of the Taovaya bois d'arc bow and their hunting tactics is the only one that exists. This method of "blitzing" a buffalo herd was called a "surround." George Catlin offers a fuller account of it among the Minatarees in 1832 (the illustration of which appears here). A surround began when two lines of horsemen, about a mile distant from one another, advanced on either side of a herd and slowly brought their ends together to encircle the animals. "Whilst the poor affrighted animals were eddying about in a crowded and confused mass, hooking and climbing upon each other," Catlin mounted a rise to watch "the work of death." He continues: "In this grand turmoil, a cloud of dust was soon raised, which in parts obscured the throng where the hunters were galloping their horses around and driving the whizzing arrows or their long lances to the hearts of these noble animals. . . . In this way the grand hunt soon resolved itself into a desperate battle; and in the space of fifteen minutes, resulted in the total destruction of the whole herd . . ." (George Catlin, *Letters and Notes on the Manners, Customs, and Conditions of North American Indians*, I, 199–200).

32. The brutal treatment of prisoners was often the one major negative in early European reports of the Taovaya-Wichitas and earned them a reputation for cruelty. "Sad it is that the good seen in these Indians serves only as a counterweight for their evil inclinations, such as the barbarous treatment of their captives . . ." was de Mézières's reaction (Bolton, *Athanase de Mézières*, I, 295). Similarly, Gaignard spoke of "the atrocities which their prisoners experience at their hands, which are so great that even to relate them would cause horror, and make the narrator a party to them" (*Ibid.*, II, 204).

Glass, on the other hand, seems relatively nonplussed in his own reporting of these customs, and omits a judgment.

It ought to be noted that Glass evidently saw slaves still among the Taovaya-Wichitas. Before the Spaniards abolished Indian slavery in Louisiana, six years after acquiring the province, the Red River village complex had served as an Indian "slave mart," exchanging Apaches to the French hunters, who then sold them in Natchitoches to rice, sugar, and cotton planters (Smith, "The Tawéhash in Imperial Affairs," 21).

3. On the Winter Hunt, October–March, 1808–1809

1. This is Glass's first mention of the great meteorite in whose history he will now become an actor. Since the American party is known to have been interested in silver and mines, and probably brought prospecting tools, it is not difficult to guess how the conversation leading to "the mass of metal" began. Unlike the metallic meteorites in Europe, which had long since been hammered into tools or weapons, most of the New World's meteorites were still in situ when the Europeans arrived. The Texas meteorites had evidently been found by the *norteños* shortly after they transplanted the Apaches. Certain it is that by 1772, when de Mézières visited the Brazos River Tawakoni villages, at least one had been discovered—probably recently, for the excitement was high. "There is not a person in the village who does not tell of it," the Frenchman reported, describing it as "a mass of metal which the Indians say is hard, thick, heavy, and composed of iron. They venerate it as an extraordinary manifestation of nature" (Bolton, *Athanase de Mézières*, I, p. 296).

That veneration likely deepened with the arrival on the Red soon after of frequent bands of Skidi Pawnees. The Skidis, a recent scholar believes, possessed "a sky-oriented theology perhaps without parallel in human history." They actively searched for meteorites (*tahu:ru'* in their language; the same word was also used for arrow or missile), which were regarded as "very sacred." According to James Murie, the Skidi sang bundle songs "about the moon, the sun, and the stars, but the songs of the meteorite are the Pawnee's favorite, for a meteorite is a child of Tirawahat [the supreme being], that has flown down from the heavens" (Von del Chamberlain, *When Stars Came Down to Earth: Cosmology of the Skidi Pawnee Indians of North America*, 29, 44, 57, 150; Wedel, "Native Astronomy," 131–45).

2. Tatesuck is representative of a considerable group—perhaps several hundred from 1700 to the 1870s—of captured Hispanic children who were raised as plains Indians. For the Comanches and others this was a way to recover population losses and to augment band power. De Mézières had found ten New Mexico Spaniards of both sexes among the Taovayas in 1778, all bought from the Comanches (Bolton, *Athanase de Mézières*, II, 209). Sibley likewise mentioned them, and added the story of a captive daughter of a former governor-general of the Provincias Internas who had astonished the frontier by refusing to leave her Comanche band, saying that she had become "reconciled to their way of life" (Sibley, "Historical Sketches," 1082–84). As pointed out by the psychologist Abram Kardiner ("Analysis of Comanche Culture," in Kardiner et al., *The Psychological Frontiers of Society*, 96) and documented by observers such as Berlandier, Catlin, and now Glass, some compensation mechanism drove many of these acculturated Europeans to high achievement within Indian cultures. One manifestation was a pronounced contempt for their countrymen in the settlements.

3. Glass is on the move again, and we now trace him on U.S.G.S. Sherman Quadrangle, scale 1:250,000, although his movements soon take him off this map. The party

of traders and Indians is on the upper drainage of Elm Fork of the Trinity, in the vicinity of Nocona, Montague County, Texas. The camp this day is probably on Still Creek.

4. They cross Barrel Springs, East Belknap, Polecat, and Victoria creeks and probably camp on the Middle Belknap near present Bowie.

5. Probably to upper Prairie Branch of Big Sandy Creek. The reference to scarce timber clearly puts them in the scrubby edge of the Western Cross Timbers, west of Rattlesnake Mountain.

6. Glass has passed into modern Jack County, and we now locate him on U.S.G.S. Wichita Falls Quadrangle, scale 1:250,000. The Comanche encampment is near the Taovaya pony range on the waters of the West Fork of the Trinity, just above present Jacksboro.

The Comanches Glass now meets are possibly of the Nokoni ("Those Who Move Often," or "Wanderer") band, but more likely they are southern Comanches, called Penateka ("Honey-Eaters") in their language, or sometimes Ho'is ("Timber People") because of their preference for the Western Cross Timbers and Edwards Plateau country. The most southeasterly of the five principal Comanche divisions, the Penateka were the Comanches most in contact with the Spaniards in Texas and associated closely with the Taovaya-Wichitas and Caddos (Wallace and Hoebel, *The Comanches*, 25–26).

7. John Maley, who somehow found out a great deal about the Texas meteorites, says that the Indians had been impressed by the ringing noise it made when struck: "The Pawnee Indians had found it and by touching of it they heard the ring of it; they thought it to be some great spirit. . . ." (Flores, "The John Maley Journal," 44). Archaeoastronomers who have studied the Plains Caddoans believe that they were aware of all the phenomena associated with a meteorite fall. This was particularly true of the Skidi, but also of the Taovaya-Wichitas, whose "star cult" cosmology was likewise advanced according to Dorsey, *Mythology of the Wichita*, 18. Glass specifically mentions that the meteorite was a healing shrine, and later anthropologists have pointed out in this connection that night-sky meteors, known to the Taovaya-Wichitas as "The-Light-That-Flies," likewise were associated with healing (Newcomb, *Indians of Texas*, 271). Many peoples, including the ancient Greeks and Romans, shared this veneration of meteorites. As will emerge in the Epilogue, they were yet an unknown quantity in Western science (Hubert Newton, "The Worship of Meteorites," *American Journal of Science* 3 (1897): 1–14).

8. Since Professor Silliman of Yale first had the famous pioneer geographer William Darby work on the problem in the 1820s, a number of scholars have attempted to fix the location of this important early meteorite find. Darby used the latest John Melish map, based for the region in question upon Darby's own travels in the Southwest. But Darby had never gotten beyond present Louisiana, and both he and Melish placed the Taovaya-Wichita villages too far to the east. Hence Darby's collation put the meteorite at 32°20′N., 97°10′W. (Darby to Silliman, Philadelphia, February 23, 1822, Silliman Family Collection). In 1892 W. F. Cummins brought together historical materials in an attempt to locate "the three" Texas meteorites, but did not suggest a location different from Darby's. See his "The Texas Meteorites," *Transactions of the Texas Academy of Sciences* 1 (1892): 14–18.

Modern scholars of meteoritics have puzzled over the problem. Brian Mason's "Chart of U.S. Meteorites" in his work, *Meteorites*, 243, places the great meteorite in Darby's location as well—near Cleburne in present Johnson County. Max H. Hew, in *The Catalogue Of Meteorites*, 403, suggests a location in either Smith County (East Texas) or Johnson County but believes "the place of find cannot be accurately placed."

I do not agree. Based upon present archaeological knowledge of the Taovaya-Wichita site, coupled with a careful retracing of Glass's route by going over the terrain with the journal and topographic maps in hand, the location of this famous Texas meteorite can be fixed fairly accurately. I believe that when Glass "approached the place where the metal was," he was traveling across the rolling mesquite plains due east of the present town of Albany, Shackleford County. Because of their pony herds, the party's route from the Comanche encampment on the Trinity would have kept them in the grasslands west of the Cross Timbers. His reference to "a hilly broken country" must refer to the northern outcrops of the Palo Pinto Mountains, which means they crossed the Brazos somewhere north of the present Possum Kingdom impoundment. Other geologic and topographical features Glass will describe fix him on the west side of this location also. Thus the Shackleford County location, somewhere around the intersection of 32°45′N. and 99°10′W., is the logical setting for Glass's dramatic discovery. See U.S.G.S. Abilene Quadrangle, scale 1:250,000, and V. E. Barnes, *The Geologic Atlas of Texas, Abilene Sheet*, scale 1:250,000 (Bureau of Economic Geology, The University of Texas at Austin, 1972).

9. I believe he means distant from the location of this meteorite and not from the Taovaya-Wichita villages, as Silliman thought in 1824. See the epilogue for my account of the discovery and subsequent history of these other meteorites.

10. They have seen the fracture line, running north-south just beyond the Albany area, of the fault between the Wolfcampian and Leonardian geological series, laid down during the Paleozoic Era. Most of west-central Texas was underneath seas during the Silurian, Pennsylvanian, and (most recently) the Cretaceous periods. Both sandstones and fossil fauna from these strata are exposed along the fracture lines. Particularly common in this area are brachiopods and clams of the Cisco Group, dating from the Pennsylvanian seas of 300 million years ago (V. E. Barnes, *Geologic Atlas of Texas, Abilene Sheet*, and American Association of Petroleum Geologists *Geological Highway Map of Texas* [Tulsa, 1973]).

11. We have seen that William C. Alexander and John Davis are by now veterans of the prairie trade, known and liked by the Taovayas, apparently friends with several Comanche bands. One or both likely handled the languages by now, and certainly the language of trade. Now we learn that others in the party have a stake in the trade goods they have packed into this remote country. Alexander knows of a Comanche band he thinks is more likely to trade, or that has better horses, and they seem to be east of here. Nothing substantial is known of the movements of these people until mid-1809, when several of their number from both Natchez and Natchitoches will mount rival expeditions to retrieve the meteorite. Perhaps they return to have another look at it now; it is certain that some negotiations with the Indians must take place.

12. According to Josiah Gregg, no other white men were so safe and protected among Indians as traders (*Commerce of the Prairies*, II, 249).

13. Americans of the first decade of the nineteenth century knew that the Rocky Mountains (often called the "Stony," "Shining," or "Mexican" mountains) bordered the plains on the west, but most of the details were still hazy in 1808. Glass would not have known where the Rockies were relative to his route; more importantly, he would not have known what they looked like, either. For three weeks they have been traveling westerly from a remote Indian village on the prairies. Now, from the monotonous roll of the Southern Plains, a high blue uplift begins to loom to the southwest. What Glass is actually seeing through the deceptive haze of distance is not the Rockies, however, but the Callahan Divide, a juniper-covered ridge of remnant ocean limestone laid down in

Cretaceous time. Rising to a maximum elevation of 2,400 feet, about 600 feet above the Abilene Plain, the eighty-mile-long divide appears much higher because of the exaggeration of height peculiar to objects viewed across flat plains country. From Glass's position on the land, the Callahan Divide does resemble a mountain range. Background reading here included John Allen's "Geographical Knowledge and American Images of the Louisiana Territory," *Western Historical Quarterly* 1 (April, 1971): 151–70.

14. Glass does not tell us enough about his route on this stretch to enable me to fix it precisely. Either he skirted the eastern finger of the Callahan Divide or else the Indians took him through the pass between the two ridges later known as Buffalo Gap—note that he says nothing more about "the great Rocky mountains." If they went through Buffalo Gap they followed the ancient bison-Indian trace that would be used later in the nineteenth century by the Butterfield Stage line as well as many California-bound emigrant trains.

Whatever his approach to it, the pecan-lined creek Glass strikes on October 20 is undoubtedly modern Pecan Bayou, which heads on the southern slopes of the Callahan Divide. The pecan (*Carya illinoinensis*) is a characteristic native of West Texas; formerly much more widely distributed, it is confined in its range by the modern climate in semiarid Texas to stream bottoms as far west as the 101st meridian.

15. "The Comanche, like other Indians, had no moral inhibitions against gambling" (Wallace and Hoebel, *The Comanches*, 117). Gambling of all sorts was, in fact, a major pastime. This game, "Hide-the-Bullet," was one of the most popular night and winter-camp games all over the continent. Among the Comanches it commonly was a team sport, with players arranged facing one another in parallel lines, and the bullet (or some other object) was often passed between team members. Sticks were used as score counters, the game usually ending at twenty-one. Hide-the-Bullet was played to the accompaniment of boisterous game songs and bets on everything from horses and weapons to wives (Robert S. Neighbors, "The Naüni or Comanches of Texas," in Henry Rowe Schoolcraft, ed., *Information Respecting the History, Conditions, and Prospects of the Indian Tribes of the United States*, II, 133).

16. Amangual, leading his Spanish force through the country just west of here the previous spring, provides us with the possible identities of some of these chiefs and bands, since many of the more westerly bands wintered along the middle Colorado. The band Lucas and Awahakei reported seeing October 20–21 probably was Chief Cordero's band, which Amangual had found encamped in April near the confluence of the Concho and Colorado. Later described as "tall, regal," Chief Cordero had been presented a rifle as a gift from Governor Cordero. But he was destined to become a great friend of the Americans; he visited Natchitoches in 1818 and in 1821 saved a party of Americans from other Comanches. Farther west Amangual had treated with Chief Chiojas, who led a band of 200 lodges and who had tersely assured Amangual, after listening to a long harangue on the American threat, that "they were faithful to everything." Near the Llano Estacado Amangual had met two Yamparika bands, led by Ysambanbi ("Handsome Wolf") and Queque. Visinampa, a Yamparika, was one of the chiefs who had visited Sibley in 1807. One other Comanche chief specifically mentioned in the Spanish documents as suspected of entertaining the American traders was Chief Hunchinampa, a Yamparika from the upper Colorado (Francisco Amangual, "Diary of Francisco Amangual from San Antonio to Santa Fe, March 30–May [June] 19, 1808," entries for April 12–13, April 22–25, May 4 and 17, in Loomis and Nasatir, *Pedro Vial*, 467 and n. 11, 468, 472–73, 479, 489–90). For more about Hunchinampa, see the epilogue.

17. Farther east during this same period interesting developments have taken

place. In mid-October, just three days before Antonio Cordero relinquished his three-year appointment as governor of Texas to young Manuel de Salcedo (nephew of the commandant of the Provincias Internas), a contingent of Taovayas, Wichitas, and Skidis from the Red River villages arrived in San Antonio and soon admitted that Glass's party of traders had come among them. They also reported that a part of yet another party of Louisianians, who had that summer traveled north of their villages bound for New Mexico and the Yamparika bands, recently had passed through their country on the return trip (Cordero to N. Salcedo, San Antonio, October 11, 1808; Nemecio Salcedo to Cordero, Chihuahua, November 29, 1808, the Bexar Archives). Perhaps the returning traders were with Jacques Clamorgan, who had reached Santa Fe from Saint Louis in December, 1807, and is known to have returned to Natchitoches along the line of the Red River in 1808 (Loomis and Nasatir, *Pedro Vial*, 248).

Portentously for the new governor, the pressing problems facing him as he took office involved the American encroachment. Two weeks later (late October), troops from the Nacogdoches garrison took as prisoner an Ais (Caddo) who was bound for Natchitoches with the letter to Sibley (dated September 15) that Glass had turned over to the Nadako for delivery. The intercepted letter was forwarded on to San Antonio and then to Chihuahua, where Salcedo stressed in response that San Antonio officials must make it clear to the Texas Indians that Spain was offended by their intercourse with Glass. In the meantime, Texas officials scrambled to find trade goods to keep the Red River tribes away from the Americans (See Guadiana to Cordero, Nacogdoches, November 10, 1808; Nemecio Salcedo to Cordero, Chihuahua, November 29, 1808, the Bexar Archives).

18. There had been no "battle" between American and Spanish troops, but during the first week of November Sibley had perpetrated a highly significant incident of "aggression" in the trade war between the two powers. In what appears to have been a calculated move, he first allowed Samuel Davenport to purchase goods in Natchitoches, a routine practice for more than a decade. Then, as Davenport approached the Neutral Ground on his return trip to Nacogdoches, Sibley had American troops arrest him and charge him with violation of the 1807 Embargo Act. All of Davenport's trade goods were confiscated. This "cart incident" as the Spaniards would call it became the subject of much angry correspondence between Spanish officials in the winter of 1808–1809. Since the Nacogdoches trading house recently had contracted to supply San Antonio with its complete stock of goods for the Texas trade, this event will lead to a crisis at that capital. Spanish officials were convinced that Sibley was attempting to leave Texas Indians no choice but to trade with the Americans (Manuel Salcedo to Cordero, San Antonio, November 30, 1808, the Bexar Archives). See the epilogue.

19. Lipan Apaches. The Lipans were the Athapaskan speakers whom Coronado had encountered as plains bison hunters whose products were transported via dog caravans. The advance of the prairie Caddoans and the Comanches into Texas had driven these Eastern Apaches south and west; during this period only a small remnant of Lipans was living at Mission San Antonio de Valero (the Alamo), where they sought Spanish protection. In March of 1807 Cordero had sought a peace between the Lipans and the Comanches and Tawakonis, but from the lukewarm reception two Lipan messengers received, the Indians with Glass obviously did not have their hearts in it. By 1809 Goseascochea would report that whatever peace existed did not last: the Tawakonis and Comanches had by then invited the Taovayas to join them against the Lipans (Cordero to N. Salcedo, San Antonio, March 31, 1807; and Goseascochea, "Diary," entry for November 4, 1809, both in the Bexar Archives). For a solid, firsthand ethnographic account of the Texas Lipans, see Berlandier, *The Indians of Texas in 1830*, 128–35.

20. Glass has been taken on the traditional winter round of the Taovayas and Pena-teka Comanches, into their favorite wintering country on the middle Colorado, where numerous Indian bands annually congregated to hunt and trade from November to March to take advantage of the consolidation of wintering plains wildlife in the sheltered valleys and woods of the Texas Hill Country.

Since he makes no journal entries between October 28 and December 7, during their winter camps along the Colorado, however, their route here can only be extrapolated from the few details he does provide. The two previous scholars who have examined the Glass journal, Elizabeth John and William Goetzmann, are of little help here. John makes no attempt to trace Glass's route at all, believing it cannot be done (see her "Portrait of a Wichita Village, 1808," *Chronicles of Oklahoma* 60 (Winter, 1892–83): 436 n. 28). Goetzmann, in his Pulitzer Prize–winning *Exploration and Empire: The Explorer and the Scientist in the Winning of the West,* 54, assumes that the Indians took Glass *up*stream, to the vicinity of Big Spring, Texas. Once again, however, Glass can be followed only by taking his journal into the countryside and matching his descriptions with Texas topography. He will shortly describe the Colorado River as about fifty yards wide and rocky—unquestionably, then, he traveled *down* the Colorado, at least to Gorman Falls and probably downstream as far as present Lake Buchanan, where the Hill Country phase of the Colorado does assume those characteristics. See U.S.G.S. Brownwood and Llano Quadrangles, scale 1:250,000, to trace his winter route along the Colorado River, which they will now leave.

21. There are no corroborative documents for this assassination plan in the Bexar Archives, but it is unlikely that there would be. Since the plan is consistent with the contemporary Spanish policy vis-a-vis American traders (i.e., avoiding "noisy disturbances" with the U.S. government), I suspect that the idea did originate as an oral order in San Antonio and that it did place Glass in serious jeopardy. If the plan had been successful, Glass's death could then have been blamed on an Indian. Tatesuck's actions make it likely that he had established a kinship tie with Glass—especially likely if, as earlier suggestions indicate, Glass had shared his wife. This was a common protective device in trade. See W. Raymond Wood, "Contrastive Features of Native North American Trade Systems," in *Oregon University Anthropological Papers*, No. 4, 162.

22. To the north of the country inhabited by the Penateka and the Nokoni (and those smaller Comanche bands such as the Tanima, or Liver-Eaters, and the Tenewa, or Down-Streams, who shared the Central Texas country with them), the Comanchería was inhabited by three important divisions. Immediately to the northwest were the Kwaharena or Kwahadi, a name that means "Antelopes." They occupied the pronghorn country atop the Llano Estacado. The Kutsueka or Buffalo-Eaters, whose eastern bands were sometimes called the "Texas Comanches" by the Spaniards, ranged between the Red and Canadian rivers. Strung over a great distance to the west of these were the Yamparika, or Yap-Eaters, the last of the Shoshonean peoples to leave the Central Rockies and become plains Comanches. Wallace and Hoebel, *The Comanches,* 26–31, mention another dozen or more smaller bands in addition to these.

23. His observations are valuable, but his conclusions anthropologically faulty here. Comanche domination of West Texas during Glass's time seems to have been so secure that the winter hunting parties took along only enough women to do camp work and to keep things interesting sexually. This, not frequent murder of Comanche women, explains the different ratios of women among the two peoples.

A young Comanche woman was accorded the same sexual freedom before marriage as men enjoyed, but extramarital sex without the permission (or encouragement) of her husband was culturally punishable. However, there is evidence that as Comanche culture evolved into its plains form, emphasizing male hunting and war prowess and female subservience, female rebellion began to express itself sexually, causing considerable anxiety among prestige-conscious Comanche males. Even so, Glass has witnessed an extraordinary event. Despite tension between the sexes, Comanche culture as later reported sought to avoid interband hostility between warriors. In all forty-five cases of female infidelity remembered by Wallace and Hoebel's informants, cuckolded Comanche husbands directed their anger at their wives (most were disfigured; seven were killed) but merely demanded material restitution from their lovers. In this later era, none of the males was remembered as having been attacked (Wallace and Hoebel, *The Comanches*, 225, 232–34; Berlandier, *The Indians of Texas in 1830*, 118; and especially a psychological study, Kardiner's "Analysis of Comanche Culture," 89–95).

24. Sibley reported that during his council with the Comanches in August of 1807, so many horses were brought into Natchitoches that "the Commons" could not support them. Accordingly, he had hired three men to take the herd to another pasture, since "the Hietans who have the Most Horses being Accustom'd to Praries & no woodsmen, in searching their Horses in the woods would probably get lost themselves." It was a gesture the Indians understood, but it had backfired when a storm stampeded the herd and they broke through the pen. Twenty-five Indian ponies turned up missing and were believed stolen. Sibley had endeavored to atone for this inadvertent breach of faith, but the Comanches had been upset, and Glass now suffers the retaliation (Sibley, *Report From Natchitoches*, entries for August 13 and 18, pp. 50, 56).

25. On December 11 Glass's party left the Colorado River, along which they had traveled and camped for more than a month, and struck out to the northeast. By December 19 they have arrived at the Brazos, from which camp Glass pens this December 30 entry, a digression on the country he has seen since early November. Their route from the Colorado can only be approximated from the few clues he does offer—one of which is his description of this "pyramid mount."

This has been an elusive landmark to locate, principally because of an error in the journal, probably made when it was copied. Comanche Peak in Hood County seems a plausible choice looking at a topographical map (it is near the Brazos, albeit *west* of the river), but on the ground this long, flat-topped mesa bears no resemblance to what Glass describes. East of the Brazos, no peaks at all thrust up from the Grand Prairie.

The explanation struck me while leafing through Earl Thollander's *Back Roads of Texas*. The author-artist includes a sketch of one of the Twin Mountains northwest of today's Lampasas and some ten or twelve miles east of the *Colorado* river. A trip into the area in May, 1983, confirmed my suspicion that in locating this "pyramid," either Glass or the copyist had written "Brassos" when "Colorado" was meant.

The Lampasas Cut Plain lying northeast of the middle Colorado is indeed an "extensive Knobby Prarie," which features nearly a dozen roughly pyramidal peaks—including San Saba Peak, Waters Mountain, Cedar Top Peak, the Twin Sisters, Flat Top Peak, Boys Peak, the Twin Mountains, Onion Top, and Castle Peak. These are outlying erosion cones whose summits (as Glass relates for the one he climbed) are capped with remnant Fredricksburg limestone. Katie Dowdy, Dale Henry of Austin, and I have probably established some sort of Texas mountain climbing record in an unsuccessful search for the cistern from which Glass drank in 1808. Our conclusion is that 200-foot-high Boys Peak, which my husky dog, Kooa, and I climbed in 1983, is the most likely choice. Its situation is closest to what the journal describes, but at present the cap on top is too broken by weathering to catch water. See Robert Sheldon, *Roadside Geology of*

Texas, 113–15; also, U.S.G.S. 7.5' topographic maps for Goldthwaite, Nix, Flat Top Peak, Adamsville, Ogles, and Castle Peak.

26. They traveled, apparently from the Lampasas Cut Plain across the northern reaches of the Comanche Plateau ("generally hilly Limestone in abundance") to the point where the Brazos emerges from the Cross Timbers onto the Grand Prairie. Perhaps Nolan had made this round with the Indians in the early 1790s. But Glass is the first American to leave a written account of this remote part of west-central Texas. He was not a trained observer and does not, indeed, tell us much about the country—although at least two cartographers will use his journal in preparing their maps (see the epilogue). His frequent allusions to "most excellent Pasturage" and the scarcity of woody growth evoke images of the appearance of this Texas landscape when it was fire-managed by the Indians for hunting and pasturage. When later Anglo ranchers fenced and overstocked these counties, suppressing the natural fire ecology, the native grasslands rapidly were taken over by broomweed, junipers, and mesquite. See Robin Doughty, *Wildlife and Man in Texas*, 121; Carl C. Wright, "The Mesquite Tree: From Nature's Boon to Aggressive Invader," *Southwestern Historical Quarterly* 69 (1965): 38–43; Dan Flores, "Indian Utilization of Range Resources in Texas" (paper read at the Twentieth Annual Range Management Conference, Lubbock, Texas, 1983, in possession of the author).

27. On one of his wide-ranging forays, Philip Nolan crossed and left a description (see the introduction) of these "high lands." Glass does not see the headwaters of either river, but interestingly in view of his earlier "great Rocky mountains" comment, he (correctly) does not place them in mountains. Later travelers, most notably the Texan Santa Fe party of 1841, saw mountains at the headwaters of the Brazos. But, as trader Gregg knew from experience, these were "without doubt the *cejas* or brows of the elevated table plains . . . which, when viewed from the plain below, often assume the appearance of formidable mountains; but once upon their summit the spectator sees another vast plain before him" (Gregg, *Commerce of the Prairies*, II, 180). Only in the late nineteenth century did the complete image of the Llano Estacado plain as a drainage divide and origin for the Red, Brazos, and Colorado rivers finally materialize.

28. See section 2, n. 14.

29. As with all his river characterizations, this one is accurate. The Sabine River originates in the Blackland Prairie of present Collin and Hunt counties, Texas. Glass is providing many geographical details not previously known to Americans. The title of his journal gives reason to believe that Glass will descend the Sabine on his return trip to Natchitoches.

30. Since he is not carrying instruments of celestial observation, this latitude figure is only a guess and probably represents a climate comparison with Natchez and Natchitoches. Glass's party seems to wander around quite a bit during this period in search of grass and mustang herds, and since there are no entries in his journal between December 30 and February 6, I must extrapolate his route from the few clues he provides. Judging from this latitude figure, his terse comments (bison and mustangs "seen by the thousands," the country "elevated and open," and—later—apprehension of a "Tanverata" attack), along with Philip Nolan's known preferences in horse-catching country, Glass's six weeks of mustanging almost certainly took place in the Grand Prairie, probably in the area just south of present Fort Worth.

31. Like so much of the horse-working culture of the Southwest, the technique of catching large numbers of wild horses came from the Hispanics, in this case the *mesteñeros* ("mustangers" who may themselves have borrowed the basic idea from the Indian technique of impounding pronghorns). We have seen that Glass uses Spanish ter-

minology; these early traders may also have called the mustang pen by its Spanish name—*coral de adventura*. Commonly it was a spiral-shaped pen, fifty to sixty feet in diameter, built of mesquite posts five to six feet high lashed together with rawhide thongs. This made a strong but elastic fence whose spiral shape tended to sweep a running herd into a mill in the center. Two brush wings fanned out half a mile or more from the corral; successfully driving a *mañada*, or drove, into this funnel started the action. The pen had to be situated strategically on the land and at least partially concealed. Glass's explanation for their failures is evocative—too many bison. See G. C. Robinson, "Mustangs and Mustanging in Southwest Texas," and J. C. Moses, "A Mustanger of 1850," both in J. Frank Dobie et al., eds., *Mustangs and Cow Horses*, 5–6, 39–41.

32. Glass here offers an early firsthand observation useful to grassland ecologists: that localized overgrazing by bison and other herd animals was part of the natural cycle on the Great Plains. For an intriguing discussion that illuminates some of the possible consequences, see Floyd Larson's "The Role of the Bison in Maintaining the Short Grass Plains," *Ecology* 21 (April, 1940): 113–21.

33. They are retracing their route of early October now, traversing the rolling Western Cross Timbers in North Texas.

34. See section 2, n. 17.

35. Add to Glass's losses via Indian theft another thirty-six animals taken by the Osages and he has lost nearly eighty horses altogether. It is unfortunate that he does not tell us how many head he will finally drive back to Mississippi. See Sibley to Eustis, Natchitoches, May 10, 1809, in Garrett, "Doctor John Sibley," 47 (January, 1944): 323. Interestingly, the Spaniards will contend that the horses traded to Glass were themselves stolen—from the Lipans (Bernardo Bonavía to Nicolás Benítez, San Antonio, October 20, 1809, the Bexar Archives).

36. Glass's own contribution to "his" journal ends with his departure from the Taovaya-Wichita villages in March of 1809. Evidently dissatisfied with Glass's comments on the Comanches, Sibley at this point has appended to the journal his own observations in this section titled "Character of the Hietan Indians"—the first recorded comments by an American we have on these Indians. See Sibley to Silliman, Natchitoches, June 2, 1822, the Silliman Family Collection. As with the "Song of the Orphan" migration tradition, the addition seems to spring from Sibley's conviction that the Glass journal would be published. Unlike the earlier insertion, however, this end section is not original: the same comments, in slightly different form, appear in Sibley's letters to the War Department following the Great Council of 1807. These comments have been published and annotated by Annie Heloise Abel in Sibley's *A Report from Natchitoches in 1807*, 76–80. I confine my annotation here to remarks illuminated by more recent scholarship.

37. Sibley is advancing range and population figures for the Comanches that would have made them the most numerous and widespread Indians of North America. Only by including all other Shoshonean speakers—Utes, Paiutes, Shoshones, and so on—however, is this extensive a range accurate. The Comanchería proper was much more narrowly defined, extending from the Eastern Cross Timbers west to the Pecos River and from the Texas Hill Country north to the Arkansas River. Wallace and Hoebel's informants remembered at least thirteen large Comanche bands and several smaller ones about which little is known. Relying upon James Mooney's estimates and some careful ancillary work, these scholars estimated an early nineteenth-century population of 12,000–15,000 Comanches (see *The Comanches*, 12, 25–26, 31–32). More recent ecological and population models indicate that the Comanchería was probably incapable of supporting a hunting population of more than about 7,000 souls without resort to exten-

sive raiding into distant regions. (Bill Brown, "Application of Thompson's [Ecological] Model to the Comanche," unpublished paper, 1982, in possession of Dan L. Flores).

38. An interesting comment on the motive for Comanche nomadism. Sibley seems to have acquired the impression that plains nomadism was more a function of stock herding than bison hunting, a point reinforced by Glass's firsthand experiences recorded in the Journal, section 3.

39. Sibley has here added several additional comments to his original 1807 observations. His early description of the Comanches seems oddly at variance with those of later observers such as Catlin, who saw the Comanches as a short, dark-complexioned people inclined towards corpulency (Catlin, *Letters and Notes*, II, 66). Despite the protestations of the Comanche chief, one explanation is that the Comanches by the early nineteenth century have been raiding Spanish settlements and stealing and adopting European children for almost a century; the other is that Sibley certainly is exaggerating.

40. Observers never tired of comparing the hard-working Indian women with the more sheltered Euroamerican female of "polite society." As bison hunters, the Comanches had a culture forged upon a sexual division of labor that—whether interpreted in anthropological or modern feminist terms—rarely allowed women to escape the role of subordinate and inferior. Since the Comanche male contributed through the hunt more than 80 percent of the food requirement, the Comanche woman performed every other task that could be done simultaneously with child care. The only exceptions were for young women, normally relieved of heavy work to be free to amuse the men, and post-menopausal women, who were free to acquire "power" and parity once their sexual value (and potential for causing strife) was gone (Wallace and Hoebel, *The Comanches*, 31—32; Ralph Linton, "The Comanche," 76–77; Gustav Carlson and Volney Jones, "Some Notes on the Uses of Plants by the Comanche Indians," *Papers of the Michigan Academy of Sciences, Arts, and Letters* 25 (1940): 517–20.

Part 3. Epilogue

1. Thomas Linnard, Natchitoches–Sulphur Fork Agency Ledgers, ledger entry for August 26, 1809, the National Archives.

2. Skidi tradition collected by James Murie, quoted in Chamberlain, *When Stars Came Down To Earth*, 146.

3. Sibley to Eustis, Natchitoches, May 10, 1809, in Garrett, "Doctor John Sibley," 47 (January, 1944): 322–23.

4. For a discussion, see J. Frank Dobie, *Coronado's Children: Tales of Lost Mines and Buried Treasures of the Southwest*, 4–6.

5. See Flores, *Jefferson and Southwestern Exploration*, 15, 17, and n. 19.

6. Mason, *Meteorites*, 3–5.

7. "Fall of Meteoric Stones in Connecticut," *Medical Repository* 5, no. 2 (1808): 202–13; Barbara Narenda, "The Peabody Museum Meteorite Collection: A Historic Account," *Discovery* 13 (1978): 11; John C. Greene, *American Science in the Age of Jefferson*, 148–51.

8. Sibley to Eustis, Natchitoches, May 10, 1809, in Garrett, "Doctor John Sibley," 47 (January, 1944): 321–22; Linnard, Natchitoches–Sulphur Fork Agency Ledgers, ledger entry for August 26, 1809. For some reason, years later Sibley told Benjamin Silliman that "No piece of similar Metal was ever Sent from here to Philad.—" (Sibley to Silliman, Natchitoches, June 2, 1822, Silliman Family Collection). This is one of a

number of strange inconsistencies in Sibley's testimony concerning the meteorite and its retrieval.

9. Sibley's version is in the Silliman Family Collection and was written more than a decade after the events. John Maley's account, written sometime between 1815 and 1819, was derived from conversations with the traders involved. The two versions are close but not identical to one another. The third document is Captain José de Goseascochea's Diary, October 5 to November 21, 1809, the Bexar Archives, tersely recording the travels of the cavalry patrol he commanded during its search for the Americans.

10. Bill McWilliams was in Concordia Parish, homesteading on the west bank of the Mississippi, before 1811. Later he would show up in the American colonies in Texas, where he was known as "an old Comanche trader" with knowledge of the country and of "mines" in the Texas outback (see note 37 below). Piper probably was Gilbert (Guillermo, or William) Piper, a Feliciana Parish homesteader who took up a claim near the Mississippi in 1806. Several John Smiths signed squatter's petitions in the Natchez region during this period, and at least two were in the Natchitoches area. Dungeon and Corvis cannot be located in the land documents, and I have made no attempt to trace them down in the manuscript censuses. See the *American State Papers: Public Lands*, Louisiana land claims, 2, p. 672, and 4, p. 445.

11. According to Maley's account (Flores, "The John Maley Journal," 46–50), as well as Sibley to Amos Stoddard, Natchitoches, April 2, 1812, in the Sibley Papers, Manuscript Department, Missouri Historical Society, Saint Louis, wherein he writes: "I am impatient to hear your opinion of the Piece [of] Mineral Sent to New York by Mr. Johnston, in which I have an interest."

It might be noted that Sibley never made a report to his superiors in Washington on the expeditions to retrieve the meteorite and that in 1822 he insisted to Benjamin Silliman (Sibley to Silliman, Natchitoches, June 2, 1822, Silliman Family Collection) that "other gentlemen" furnished "the outfit of goods" to purchase the meteorite.

12. Flores, "John Maley Journal," 46–47.

13. Sibley's letter says the second party was formed at Nacogdoches, but that cannot be, as that city was Spanish in 1809. Almost certainly Sibley's reference to Nacogdoches is an error, and he meant Natchez.

14. The Davis party seems to have been peopled largely by early Anglo settlers in the disputed border region of West Florida, within four years to be the scene of a revolution against Spanish control. Aaron Robinson (whom Sibley calls "Edward") was a settler in the Feliciana region in 1808. Edmund Quirk was of questionable location in 1809, but by 1825 he would claim a section of land in the old Neutral Ground (a former haunt?) within eight miles of the Sabine River. Knowland was another Feliciana Parish man who had settled there under a Spanish grant in 1803. There was also a Skinner family living in the area near Baton Rouge between 1807 and 1814, although no "William" is mentioned. James White was in 1809 a Claiborne County, Mississippi Territory, resident. See the *American State Papers: Public Lands*, Louisiana and Mississippi land claims, here listed sequentially for the names above: 3, p. 68; 4, p. 101; 3, p. 390; 3, p. 40; and for White, a Memorial to the President by the Residents of Mississippi Territory, *Territorial Papers*, V, 645.

15. Bonavía to N. Salcedo, San Antonio, October 4, 1809, Bonavía to Goseascochea, San Antonio, October 4, 1809, Statement of Supplies and Horses for the Expedition, October 4, 1809, and Manuel Salcedo to Bonavía, October 6, 1809, the Bexar Archives. Brigadier General Bernardo Bonavía, governor of Durango, had arrived in San Antonio

the previous March in an effort to strengthen Texas defenses. He quickly emerged as one of the leading spirits in the opposition to American encroachments.

16. Sibley to Silliman, Natchitoches, June 2, 1822, Silliman Family Collection; Flores, "John Maley Journal," 48.

17. José de Goseascochea, "Diary Written by Captain D. José de Goseascochea of the Incidents and War Operations Incurred by the 52 men . . . [between October 5 and November 21, 1809]," the Bexar Archives. Maley's version has a Spanish patrol, not Indians, stealing the horses. Maley must have been confused on this point, but this may be evidence that the Americans knew they had been pursued by Goseascochea's troops.

18. John Sibley, "Diary," III (1809–1811), Lindenwood Collection, Missouri Historical Society, Saint Louis.

19. Flores, "John Maley Journal," 49.

20. Darby to Silliman, Philadelphia, February 28, 1822, Silliman Family Collection.

21. See Luis de Onís to Manuel Salcedo, Washington, October 21, 1809; Pedro López Prieto to Manuel Salcedo, Trinidad, December 22, 1809. My account of the Spanish resistance to American encroachments during 1809 and 1810 is a summary of these documents, all from the Bexar Archives: Bonavía to Benítez, San Antonio, October 20, 1809, and Benítez to Bonavía, Arroyo de Paiaiai, November 11, 1809; Bonavía to M. Salcedo, San Antonio, January 4, 1810; Bonavía to N. Salcedo, San Antonio, January 10, 1810; M. Salcedo to Bonavía, San Antonio, February 19, 1810; M. Salcedo to Guadiana, San Antonio, January 14, 1810; M. Salcedo to Bonavía, San Antonio, September 29, 1809; M. Salcedo's address to representatives of the Brazos–Red River tribes, San Antonio, January 31, 1810. See, also, Haggard, "House of Barr and Davenport," 76.

22. The standard treatments of the filibusters are Julia Kathryn Garrett, *Green Flag over Texas*, and Harris Gaylord Warren, *The Sword Was Their Passport: A History of American Filibustering in the Mexican Revolution*. For the Spanish response to the American threat during this period, see also two highly useful newer studies: Félix D. Almaráz, Jr., *Tragic Cavalier: Governor Manuel Salcedo of Texas, 1808–1813*, and Abraham P. Nasatir, *Borderland in Retreat: From Spanish Louisiana to the Far Southwest*.

23. On Awahakei's death and the breakup of the villages, see Sibley to Eustis, Natchitoches, December 31, 1811, in Garrett, "Doctor John Sibley," 49 (January, 1946): 413. The quote is from Chamberlain, *When Stars Came Down to Earth*, 144, but see also Wedel, "Native Astronomy and the Plains Caddoans," 132. The Great Comet of 1811, the most widely observed comet between 1759 and 1836, appeared over Europe in March and was still being observed in North America the following autumn. See Brian G. Marsden, *Catalog of Cometary Orbits*, 9–11, 31; Greene, *American Science in the Age of Jefferson*, 152.

24. See Haggard, "House of Barr and Davenport," 82–86.

25. Ora Brooks Peake, *A History of the United States Indian Factory System, 1795–1822*, 17–18, 31.

26. The best study of the American penetration into the Southwest from Saint Louis during the period between Clamorgan and William Becknell is Loomis and Nasatir, *Pedro Vial*, 248–61. I do not, of course, imply that *no* trade took place in Texas between Americans and the Plains tribes after 1810. Certainly, as American squatters settled in the Arkansas Territory, particularly at Pecan Point on the Red, and in northeast Texas, individuals and small groups of hunters must have struck up trade relations with peoples to the west. Berlandier does mention American traders among Texas Indians in the 1820s but says that the trade was small, mostly involving ammunition. "Aguajes," the

Spanish rendering of the Caddoan *Awah:i*, rather than "Owaheys," was the common frontier spelling by his day (Berlandier, *The Indians of Texas in 1830*, 119).

27. My information is from Mary Louise Hendricks, comp., *Mississippi Court Records, 1795–1835*, Warren County, Mississippi, Manuscript Census, 1810 and 1820; Haskell Monroe, Jr., and James McIntosh, eds., *The Papers of Jefferson Davis*, II, 492 n. 17; telephone interview with Mrs. Ceress Newall, Spartanburg, South Carolina, December 12, 1982.

28. Sibley to Silliman, Natchitoches, June 2, 1822; Darby to Silliman, Philadelphia, February 28, 1822, Silliman Family Collection. Carl I. Wheat, comp., *1540–1861: Mapping the Transmississippi West*, II, 67–68 and notes, discusses the maps involved here. Despite their historical importance (the Melish map was used in the Adams-Onís Treaty), he has a low opinion of them.

29. The first scientific notice, along with a drawing, of the meteorite appeared in "Mass of Malleable Iron," *Bruce's American Mineralogical Journal* 1 (1814): 124. The report of an experiment by Silliman that proved the mass's meteoric origin appeared in the same issue, pp. 218–21, in a letter by Col. George Gibbs entitled "Observations on the Mass of Iron from Louisiana." These notices are also available elsewhere, principally quoted in Charles Hunt, "Notice of the Malleable Iron of Louisiana," *American Journal of Science and Arts* 8 (1824): 219.

30. Hunt, "Notice of the Malleable Iron," 225. This 1824 article provides as full a history of the meteorite as could be assembled at that time. It incorporated material from both Glass and Maley journals, both which were assumed by Silliman and Hunt to be legitimate, firsthand accounts. The editors actively encouraged retrieval of any remaining masses, but in the interest of science rather than pecuniary gain, as "there can be no reasonable doubt that the huge masses of malleable iron from Louisiana are of meteoric origin" (224).

31. Additional articles or notices on the meteorite appeared in the *American Journal of Science and Arts* in 1829, 1835, 1838, 1846, and 1876. See C. U. Shepard, "Analysis of the Meteoric Iron of Louisiana," 16 (1829): 217; Benjamin Silliman, "Great Mass of Meteoric Iron from Louisiana," 27 (1835): 382; [Benjamin Silliman, Jr.], "Meteoric Iron in Texas," 33 (1838): 257; Benjamin Silliman, Jr., and T. S. Hunt, "On the Meteoric Iron of Texas and Lockport," ser. 2, 2 (1846): 370–76; A. W. Wright, "Tests Conducted on the Meteoric Iron of Texas," ser. 2, 11 (1876): 257.

32. Oliver Cummings Farrington, *Meteorites: Their Structure, Composition, and Terrestrial Relations*, 60, 78–80, 92–93, 201–202, is the source of my more general information here. This early, much-cited study also explains why the great meteorite did not appear oxidized. Apparently it was a fairly recent (probably within half a century) fall and was still protected from rusting by a magnetite veneer called a "fusion crust."

33. William Johnson to Silliman, Charleston, August 18, 1821, Silliman Family Collection.

34. Hunt, "Notice of the Malleable Iron," 219 n. 4; George Gates Raddin, Jr., *The New York of Hocquet Caritat and His Associates, 1797–1817*, 137–40.

35. William Goetzmann, who discovered the Maley journal while writing his dissertation at Yale, has cautioned historians "to accept his story only on the most tentative basis subject to confirmation or denial by further detailed research" (*Exploration and Empire*, 54–55). My own work editing the Maley account for a master's thesis proved the wisdom of Goetzmann's warning and has convinced me that Maley's two claimed expeditions onto the plains are fabrications. His "journal" is a product of interviews and research rather than experience, and scholars are to be warned that his geography, in par-

ticular, is garbled. Even so, what the document actually represents makes it highly interesting to historians, and someday it should be published for that reason. An exchange of correspondence with Professor Goetzmann in the fall of 1983 was very helpful in the formulation of my interpretation here. My earlier struggle with this "interesting can of worms," as Elizabeth A. H. John has described the Maley account, appears in the introduction to Flores, "John Maley Journal."

36. The story is related in J. H. Kuykendall, "Reminiscences of Early Texans: A Collection from the Austin Papers," *Texas Historical Association Quarterly* 6 (January, 1903): 249–50.

37. According to Mason's chart, "Meteorites of the United States," in *Meteorites*, 231–47.

38. Robert Neighbors to Elisha Pease, Brazos Agency, June 4, 1856, in the Papers of Elisha M. Pease, Governors' Papers, Texas State Archives, Austin; B. F. Shumard, "Notice of Meteoric Iron from Texas," *Transactions of the Academy of Science of St. Louis* 1 (1857): 622–23. Shumard incorrectly cites the date of its retrieval as 1836.

Catlin, who made his first expedition onto the Southern Plains in 1834, remained for several weeks about a Comanche village twenty-five or so miles north of this meteorite's location, which was only a few hundred yards south of the Red River, above present Electra in Wichita County, Texas. His painting of "The Comanches giving the arrows to the Medicine Rock, for success in war," possibly is of the Neighbors meteorite, which was also called Ta-pic-ta-car-re—"Standing Rock." See Catlin, *Letters and Notes* II, Letters 40–43; Hey, *Catalogue of Meteorites*, 518.

In 1896 W. F. Cummins in his "The Texas Meteorites" was the first to speculate in print that the Neighbors meteorite must have been one of the remaining pieces the Indians had mentioned to Glass.

39. The Comanche Iron, an octahedrite, was found near 31°54′N. and 98°30′W., about sixty miles from where I believe Glass was conducted to the great meteorite in 1808. See Mason, "Meteorites of the United States," in *Meteorites*, 242. A number of other early travelers in Texas mentioned masses of "native iron," among them L. Bringier, who claimed to have seen "several blocks of native iron" near the "headwaters" of the Trinity (his computation was 32°7′N. and 95°10′W.) in 1812. Another was a Robert Cox, who in 1829 wrote that he knew of "a gentleman" who had been shown a four-foot mass in Texas that he and his companions had concluded was gold (Hunt, "Notice of the Malleable Iron," 223 and note; [Silliman, Jr.], "Meteoric Iron in Texas," 257).

40. James Wilkinson, "Reflections on Louisiana," March 1804, quoted in James Robertson, ed., *Louisiana under the Rule of Spain, France, and the United States, 1785–1807*, II, 347. Wilkinson's original letter, once incorrectly credited to Vicente Folch, is in the Papeles Procedentes de la Isla de Cuba, Archivo General de Indias, Estados del Misisipi, Madrid.

Bibliography

PRIMARY MATERIAL

Unpublished Material

Bexar Archives. Manuscripts and translations. Barker Texas History Center, University of Texas at Austin.

Flores, Dan L., ed. "The John Maley Journal: Travels and Adventures in the American Southwest, 1810–1813." Master's thesis, Northwestern State University, Natchitoches, 1972.

Hendricks, Mary Louise, comp. Mississippi Court Records, 1795–1835. Mississippi Department of Archives and History, Jackson.

Natchitoches–Sulphur Fork Agency Ledgers, 1809–1821. Record Group T1029, National Archives, Washington, D.C.

Newall, Mrs. Ceress. Telephone interview. Spartanburg, South Carolina, December 12, 1982.

Papeles Procedentes de la Isla de Cuba, Archivo General de Indias. Madrid. Photocopies in the Southwest Collection, Texas Tech University, Lubbock.

Papers of Aaron Burr, Series I, Correspondence. The New-York Historical Society, New York.

Papers of Elisha M. Pease. Governors' Papers, Texas State Archives, Austin.

Peter Force Collection. Manuscripts Division, Library of Congress, Washington, D.C.

Sibley, John. "Diary," III (1809–11). Lindenwood Collection, Missouri Historical Society, Saint Louis.

Sibley Collection, Watson Library, Northwestern State University, Natchitoches, Louisiana.

Sibley Papers, Manuscript Department, Missouri Historical Society, Saint Louis.

Silliman Family Collection. Historical Manuscripts Collection, Sterling Memorial Library, Yale University, New Haven.

Spanish Archives of New Mexico. Southwest Collection, Texas Tech University, Lubbock.

Thomas Jefferson Papers. Manuscripts Division, Library of Congress, Washington, D.C.

U.S. Census, 1810, 1820 (Warren County, Mississippi).

War Department, Letters Received, Main Series. War Department Record Group M222, National Archives, Washington, D.C.

Published Material

Amangual, Francisco. "Diary of Francisco Amangual from San Antonio to Santa Fe, March 30–May [June] 19, 1808." In Noel Loomis and Abraham Nasatir, *Pedro Vial and the Roads to Santa Fe*, 462–508. Norman: University of Oklahoma Press, 1967.

American State Papers: Public Lands. Vol. II–IV.

Bean, Ellis P. "Memoir of Colonel Ellis P. Bean." In Henderson K. Yoakum, *History of Texas.* . . . Vol. I. New York: Redfield, 1856.

Berlandier, Jean Louis. *The Indians of Texas in 1830*. Edited by John C. Ewers; translated by Patricia Leclercq. Washington, D.C.: Smithsonian Institution Press, 1969.

Bolton, Herbert E., ed. *Athanase de Mézières and the Louisiana-Texas Frontier 1768–1780*. 2 vols. Cleveland: Arthur H. Clark, 1914.

Carter, Clarence, and John P. Bloom, comps. and eds. *The Territorial Papers of the United States*. Vols. V and VI, *The Territory of Mississippi, 1798–1817*. Vol. IX, *The Territory of Orleans, 1803–1812*. Washington: Government Printing Office, continually since 1933.

Catlin, George. *Letters and Notes on the Manners, Customs, and Conditions of North American Indians*. 2 vols. New York: Dover, 1973.

Cox, Isaac J., ed. "Memoir by the Sieur De La Tonty." In *The Journeys of Rene Robert Cavelier Sieur De La Salle* II, 1–30. New York: Allerton Book, 1922.

"[Documents] Concerning Philip Nolan." *Quarterly of the Texas State Historical Association* 7 (April, 1904): 308–17.

Dorsey, George A. *The Mythology of the Wichita*. Washington: Carnegie Institution, 1904.

Ellicott, Andrew. *The Journal of Andrew Ellicott*. 1803. Reprinted, Chicago: Quadrangle Books, 1962.

Flores, Dan L., ed. *Jefferson and Southwestern Exploration: The Freeman and Custis Accounts of the Red River Expedition of 1806*. Norman: University of Oklahoma Press, 1984.

Fragoso, Francisco. "Diary, Santa Fe to Natchitoches, June 24, 1788–August 20, 1789." In Noel Loomis and Abraham Nasatir, *Pedro Vial and the Roads to Santa Fe*, 327–48. Norman: University of Oklahoma Press, 1967.

Garrett, Julia Kathryn, ed. "Doctor John Sibley and the Louisiana Texas Frontier, 1803–1814." *Southwestern Historical Quarterly* 45–49 (1942–46).

Gregg, Josiah. *Commerce of the Prairies*. 2 vols. Ann Arbor: University Microfilms reprint, 1966.

Hackett, Charles Wilson, ed. and trans. *Pichardo's Treatise on the Limits of Louisiana and Texas*. 4 vols. Austin: University of Texas Press, 1931–46.

Jackson, Donald, ed. *The Journals of Zebulon Montgomery Pike, with Letters and Related Documents*. 2 vols. Norman: University of Oklahoma Press, 1966.

John, Elizabeth A. H., [ed.]. "Portrait of a Wichita Village, 1808." *Chronicles of Oklahoma* 60 (Winter, 1982–83): 412–37.

Kinnaird, Lawrence, ed. *Spain in the Mississippi Valley, 1765–1794.* 3 parts. Washington: Government Printing Office, 1946.

Kress, Margaret K., trans. "Diary of a Visit of Inspection of the Texas Missions Made by Fray Gaspar José de Solís in the Year 1767–1768." *Southwestern Historical Quarterly* 35 (1931): 28–76.

Kuykendall, J. H. "Reminiscences of Early Texans: A Collection from the Austin Papers." *Texas Historical Association Quarterly* 6 (January, 1903): 236–53.

McBee, May Wilson, ed. and trans. *Natchez Court Records, 1767–1805.* Library of the Mississippi Department of Archives and History, Jackson.

Monroe, Haskell, Jr., and James McIntosh, eds. *The Papers of Jefferson Davis.* 4 vols. Baton Rouge: Louisiana State University Press, 1971–.

Neighbors, Robert S. "The Naüni or Comanches of Texas." In Henry Rowe Schoolcraft, ed. *Information Respecting the History, Conditions, and Prospects of the Indian Tribes of the United States.* II, 125–34. 4 parts. Philadelphia: American Bureau of Indian Affairs, 1853.

Parker, W. B. *Notes Taken during the Expedition Commanded by Capt. R. B. Marcy, U.S.A., through Unexplored Texas in the Summer and Fall of 1854.* Introduction by George B. Ward. Austin: Texas State Historical Association, 1984.

Rowland, Eron Dunbar, comp. *Life, Letters and Papers of William Dunbar.* Jackson: Press of the Mississippi Historical Society, 1930.

———, ed. *Official Letter-Books of W. C. C. Claiborne, 1801–1816.* 6 vols. Jackson, Miss.: State Department of Archives and History, 1917.

Sibley, John. *A Report from Natchitoches in 1807.* Edited by Annie Heloise Abel. New York: Museum of the American Indian, 1922.

———. "Historical Sketches of the Several Tribes in Louisiana South of the Arkansas River and Between the Mississippi and the River Grand." *Annals of Congress,* 9th Cong., 2nd sess. (1806), 1076–1106.

Smith, Francis. "A Glimpse of the Texas Fur Trade in 1832." Edited by Eugene C. Barker. *Southwestern Historical Quarterly* 32 (1928): 279–82.

Swanton, John R. *Source Material on the History and Ethnology of the Caddo Indians,* Bureau of American Ethnology Bulletin 132. Washington: Government Printing Office, 1942.

Vial, Pedro. "Diary of Pedro Vial, Bexar to Santa Fe, October 4, 1786, to May 26, 1787." In Noel Loomis and Abraham Nasatir, *Pedro Vial and the Roads to Santa Fe,* 268–85. Norman: University of Oklahoma Press, 1967.

Wilkinson, James. *Memoirs of My Own Times.* 4 vols. 1816. Facsimile ed., New York: AMS Press.

———. "Reflections on Louisiana." In James Robertson, ed., *Louisiana under the Rule of Spain, France, and the United States, 1785–1807.* II, 323–47. Cleveland: Arthur H. Clark, 1911.

Maps

American Association of Petroleum Geologists. *Geological Highway Map of Texas.* Tulsa, 1973(?).

Barnes, V. E. *The Geologic Atlas of Texas, Abilene Sheet* (1972). Scale 1:250,000. Bureau of Economic Geology, University of Texas at Austin.

Darby, William. "Map of Louisiana" (1816). In Dan Flores, ed. "The John Maley Journal: Travels and Adventures in the American Southwest, 1810–1813," appendix 2. Master's thesis, Northwestern State University, Natchitoches, 1972.

Puelles, Fray José María de Jésus. *Mapa Geographica de las Provincias Septentrionales de esta Nueva España* (1807). Map Collection, Barker Texas History Center, University of Texas at Austin.

United States Geological Survey. 1:250,000 Series (Topographic). Abilene (Texas), Brownwood (Texas), Dallas (Texas), Llano (Texas), Sherman (Texas), Shreveport (Louisiana), Texarkana (Oklahoma-Texas), and Wichita Falls (Texas).

————. 7.5 Minute Series (Topographic). Adamsville (Texas), Castle Peak (Texas), Flat Top Peak (Texas), Goldthwaite (Texas), Marietta, East (Oklahoma), Nix (Texas), Ogles (Texas), and Spanish Fort (Oklahoma-Texas).

Newspapers

Mississippi Messenger (Natchez, Mississippi).

Natchez *Herald* (Natchez, Mississippi).

SECONDARY WORKS

Abernethy, Thomas Perkins. *The Burr Conspiracy.* New York: Oxford University Press, 1954.

Allen, John. "Geographical Knowledge and American Images of the Louisiana Territory." *Western Historical Quarterly* 1 (April, 1971): 151–70.

Almaráz, Félix D., Jr. *Tragic Cavalier: Governor Manuel Salcedo of Texas, 1808–1813.* Austin: University of Texas Press, 1971.

Bastian, Tyler. "Initial Report on the Longest Site." *Great Plains Newsletter* 3 (1966): 1–3.

Blaine, Martha Royce. "Mythology and Folklore: Their Possible Use in the Study of Plains Caddoan Origins." *Nebraska History* 60 (1979): 241–47.

Branson, Carl C. "Patterns of Oklahoma Prairie Mounds." *Oklahoma Geology Notes* 26 (1966): 263–73.

Bell, Robert E., Edward B. Jelks, and W. W. Newcomb. *A Pilot Study of Wichita Indian Archeology and Ethnohistory.* Final Report, National Science Foundation, 1967.

Biographical and Historical Memoirs of Northwest Louisiana. Nashville: Southern, 1890.

Brown, Bill. "Application of Thompson's [Ecological] Model to the Comanche." Unpublished paper, 1982. In possession of Dan L. Flores.

Carlson, Gustav, and Volney Jones. "Some Notes on the Uses of Plants by the Comanche Indians." *Papers of the Michigan Academy of Sciences, Arts, and Letters* 25 (1940): 517–42.

Carter, Harvey Lewis, and Marcia Carpenter Spencer. "Stereotypes of the Mountain Man." *Western Historical Quarterly* 6 (January, 1975): 17–32.

Chamberlain, Von del. *When Stars Came Down to Earth: Cosmology of the Skidi Pawnee Indians of North America.* Anthropological Papers No. 26. Los Altos, Calif.: Ballena Press, 1982.

Clabby, John. *The Natural History of the Horse.* London: Weidenfeld and Nicolson, 1976.

Claiborne, J. F. H. *Mississippi As a Province, Territory and State, with Biographical Notices of Eminent Citizens.* Jackson: Power and Barksdale, 1880.

Cox, Isaac Joslin. "The Louisiana-Texas Frontier." *Southwestern Historical Quarterly* 10 (July, 1906): 1–75; 17 (July, 1913): 1–42; 17 (October, 1913): 140–87.

———. *The West Florida Controversy, 1798–1813.* Reprint. Gloucester: Peter Smith, 1967.

Cummins, W. F. "The Texas Meteorites." *Transactions of the Texas Academy of Sciences* 1 (1892): 14–18.

Daniels, Jonathan. *The Devil's Backbone: The Story of the Natchez Trace.* New York: McGraw-Hill, 1962.

Din, Gilbert D., and Abraham Nasatir. *The Imperial Osages: Spanish-Indian Diplomacy in the Mississippi Valley.* Norman: University of Oklahoma Press, 1983.

Dobie, J. Frank. *Coronado's Children: Tales of Lost Mines and Buried Treasures of the Southwest.* Reprint. Austin: University of Texas Press, 1978.

———. *The Mustangs.* New York: Bramhall House, 1934.

———, et al., eds. *Mustangs and Cow Horses.* Dallas: SMU Press, 1940.

Dodge, Richard I. *The Hunting Grounds of the Great West.* London: Chatto and Windus, 1877.

Doughty, Robin. *Wildlife and Man in Texas.* College Station: Texas A&M University Press, 1983.

Farrington, Oliver Cummings. *Meteorites: Their Structure, Composition, and Terrestrial Relations.* Chicago: privately published, 1915.

Fehrenbach, T. R. *Comanches: The Destruction of a People.* New York: McGraw-Hill, 1974.

Flores, Dan. "The Ecology of the Red River in 1806: Peter Custis and Early Southwestern Natural History." *Southwestern Historical Quarterly* 88 (July, 1984): 1–42.

———. "Indian Utilization of Range Resources in Texas." Paper presented at Twentieth Annual Range Management Conference, Lubbock, 1983. In possession of author.

————. "The Red River Branch of the Alabama-Coushatta Indians: An Ethnohistory." *Southern Studies Journal* 16 (Spring, 1977): 55–72.

Garrett, Julia Kathryn. *Green Flag Over Texas.* New York: Cordova Press, 1939.

Goetzmann, William. *Exploration and Empire: The Explorer and the Scientist in the Winning of the West.* New York: W. W. Norton, 1966.

Gould, Frank. *The Grasses of Texas.* College Station: Texas A&M University Press, 1975.

Greene, John C. *American Science in the Age of Jefferson.* Ames: Iowa State University Press, 1984.

Haggard, J. Villasana. "The House of Barr and Davenport." *Southwestern Historical Quarterly* 49 (July, 1945): 65–88.

————. "The Neutral Ground between Louisiana and Texas, 1806–1821." *Louisiana Historical Quarterly* 28 (October, 1945): 1001–1128.

Haines, Francis. *Horses in America.* New York: Thomas Y. Crowell, 1971.

————. "The Northward Spread of Horses among the Plains Indians." *American Anthropologist* 40 (1938): 429–37.

————. "Where Did the Plains Indians Get Their Horses?" *American Anthropologist* 40 (1938): 112–17.

Hall, E. Raymond, and Keith R. Kelson. *The Mammals of North America.* 2 vols. New York: Ronald Press, 1959.

Hatcher, Mattie Austin. *The Opening of Texas to Foreign Settlement, 1801–1821.* University of Texas Bulletin No. 2714. Austin, 1927.

Haynes, Robert V. *The Natchez District and the American Revolution.* Jackson, Miss.: State Department of Archives and History, 1976.

Heitman, Francis B. *Historical Register and Dictionary of the United States Army.* 2 vols. Washington: Government Printing Office, 1903.

Hew, Max H. *The Catalogue of Meteorites.* Publication no. 464. London: Trustees of the British Museum [Natural History], 1966.

Hodge, Frederick Webb, ed. *Handbook of American Indians North of Mexico.* Bureau of American Ethnology Bulletin 30. 2 vols. Washington: Government Printing Office, 1907.

Hughes, Jack Thomas. "Prehistory of the Caddoan-Speaking Tribes." In *Caddoan Indians III.* New York and London: Garland, 1974.

Hunt, Charles. "Notice of the Malleable Iron of Louisiana." *American Journal of Science and Arts* 8 (1824): 218–25.

John, Elizabeth A. H. *Storms Brewed in Other Men's Worlds: The Confrontation of Indians, Spanish and French in the Southwest, 1540–1795.* College Station: Texas A&M Press, 1975.

[John], Elizabeth A. Harper. Part I: "The Taovayas Indians in Frontier Trade and Diplomacy, 1719–1768." *Chronicles of Oklahoma* 31 (1952).

————. Part II: "The Taovayas Indians in Frontier Trade and Diplomacy, 1769–1779." *Southwestern Historical Quarterly* 57 (1952): 181–201.

————. Part III: "The Taovayas Indians in Frontier Trade and Diplomacy,

1779–1835." *Panhandle-Plains Historical Review* 46 (1953): 41–72.

Jordan, Terry. "Pioneer Evaluation of Vegetation in Frontier Texas." *Southwestern Historical Quarterly* 76 (1973): 233–54.

Kardiner, Abram. "Analysis of Comanche Culture." In Abram Kardiner et al. *The Psychological Frontiers of Society*, 81–100. New York: Columbia University, 1945.

Kinnaird, Lawrence. "American Penetration into Spanish Louisiana." In Herbert E. Bolton, comp. *New Spain and the Anglo-American West: Historical Contributions Submitted to Herbert Eugene Bolton*. I, 211–37. Lancaster, Penn.: Lancaster Press, 1932.

Lamar, Howard R. *The Trader on the American Frontier: Myth's Victim*. College Station: Texas A&M University Press, 1977.

Larson, Floyd. "The Role of the Bison in Maintaining the Short Grass Plains." *Ecology* 21 (April, 1940): 113–21.

Lesser, Alexander. "Caddoan Kinship Systems." *Nebraska History* 60 (1979): 260–71.

Linton, Ralph. "Comanche Culture." In Abram Kardiner et al. *The Psychological Frontiers of Society*, 47–80. New York: Columbia University, 1945.

Lintz, Christopher. "The Southwestern Periphery of the Plains Caddoan Area." *Nebraska History* 60 (1979): 161–81.

Loomis, Noel M. "Philip Nolan's Entry in Texas in 1800." In John F. McDermott, ed. *The Spanish in the Mississippi Valley, 1762–1804*, 120–320. Urbana: University of Illinois Press, 1974.

———, and Abraham P. Nasatir, *Pedro Vial and the Roads to Santa Fe*. Norman: University of Oklahoma Press, 1967.

Lynott, Mark. "Prehistoric Bison Populations of Northcentral Texas." *Bulletin of the Texas Archeological Society* 50 (1980): 89–101.

McDonald, Jerry N. *North American Bison: Their Classification and Evolution*. Berkeley: University of California Press, 1981.

McNitt, Frank. *The Indian Traders*. Norman: University of Oklahoma Press, 1962.

Marsden, Brian G. *Catalog of Cometary Orbits*. Hillside, N.J.: Enslow, 1983.

Martin, P. S., and H. E. Wright, Jr., eds. *Pleistocene Extinctions: The Search for a Cause*. New Haven: Yale University Press, 1967.

Mason, Brian. *Meteorites*. New York: John Wiley & Sons, 1962.

Melton, F. A. "'Natural Mounds' of Northeast Texas, Southern Arkansas, and Northern Louisiana." *Oklahoma Academy of Sciences, Proceedings* 9 (1929): 119–30.

Narenda, Barbara. "The Peabody Museum Meteorite Collection: A Historic Account." *Discovery* 13 (1978): 11–23.

Nasatir, Abraham. *Borderland in Retreat: From Spanish Louisiana to the Far Southwest*. Albuquerque: University of New Mexico Press, 1976.

Newcomb, W. W., Jr. *The Indians of Texas*. Austin: University of Texas Press, 1961.

Newlin, Deborah Lamont. *The Tonkawa People: A Tribal History from Earliest Times to 1893.* Lubbock: West Texas Museum Association, 1982.

Newton, Hubert. "The Worship of Meteorites." *American Journal of Science* 3 (1897): 1–14.

Nuttall, Donald. "The American Threat to New Mexico, 1804–1822." Master's thesis, San Diego State College, 1959.

Oberholser, Harry C. *The Bird Life of Texas.* Edited by Edgar Kincaid. 2 vols. Austin: University of Texas Press, 1974.

Parks, Douglas R. "The Northern Caddoan Languages: Their Subgrouping and Time Depth." *Nebraska History* 60 (1979): 197–213.

Peake, Ora Brooks. *A History of the United States Indian Factory System, 1795–1822.* Denver: Sage Books, 1954.

Powell, William H. *List of Officers of the Army of the United States from 1779 to 1900.* New York: L. R. Hamersly, 1900.

Raddin, George Gates, Jr. *The New York of Hocquet Caritat and His Associates, 1797–1817.* Dover, N.J.: Dover Advance Press, 1953.

Rister, Carl C. "Harmful Practices of Indian Traders of the Southwest, 1865–1876." *New Mexico Historical Quarterly* 6 (July, 1931): 231–48.

Rollings, Willard. "Prairie Hegemony: An Ethnohistorical Study of the Osage, from Early Times to 1840." Ph.D. dissertation, Texas Tech University, Lubbock, 1983.

Rood, David S. *A Wichita Grammar.* New York: Garland Press, 1976.

Rothert, Otto A. *The Outlaws of Cave-in-Rock.* Cleveland: Arthur H. Clark, 1924.

Rowland, Dunbar. *History of Mississippi: The Heart of the South.* 2 vols. Chicago and Jackson: S. J. Clarke, 1925.

Saum, Lewis O. *The Fur Trader and the Indian.* Seattle: University of Washington Press, 1965.

Schilz, Thomas F. "People of the Cross Timbers: A History of the Tonkawa Indians." Ph.D. dissertation, Texas Christian University, 1983.

Sheldon, Robert A. *Roadside Geology of Texas.* Missoula: Mountain Press Publishing, 1982 edition.

Shepard, C. U. "Analysis of the Meteoric Iron of Louisiana." *American Journal of Science and Arts* 16 (1829): 217.

Shumard, B. F. "Notice of Meteoric Iron From Texas." *Transactions of the Academy of Science of St. Louis* 1 (1857): 622–23.

Silliman, Benjamin. "Great Mass of Meteoric Iron from Louisiana." *American Journal of Science and Arts* 27 (1835): 382.

[Silliman, Benjamin, Jr.] "Meteoric Iron in Texas." *American Journal of Science and Arts* 33 (1838): 257.

Silliman, Benjamin, Jr., and T. S. Hunt. "On the Meteoric Iron of Texas and Lockport." *American Journal of Science and Arts* ser 2, 2 (1846): 370–76.

Slaughter, Bob H., and Ronald Ritchie. "Pleistocene Mammals of the Clear Creek Local Fauna, Denton County, Texas." *Journal of the [SMU] Graduate Research Center* 31 (1963): 117–31.

Slaughter, Bob H., and W. L. McClure. "The Sims Bayou Local Fauna: Pleistocene of Houston, Texas." *Texas Academy of Science Journal* 17 (1965): 404–17.

Slotkin, Richard. *Regeneration through Violence: The Mythology of the American Frontier, 1600–1860.* Middleton, Conn.: Wesleyan University Press, 1973.

Smith, Ralph. "The Tawéhash in French, Spanish, English, and American Imperial Affairs." *West Texas Historical Association Yearbook* 28 (1952): 18–49.

Swanton, John R. *The Indian Tribes of North America.* Bureau of American Ethnology, Bulletin 145. Washington: Government Printing Office, 1952.

Thollander, Earl. *Back Roads of Texas.* Flagstaff: Northland Press, 1980.

Thomas, Heather Smith. *The Wild Horse Controversy.* South Brunswick and New York: A. S. Barnes, 1979.

Van Kirk, Sylvia. *"Many Tender Ties": Women in Fur-Trade Society, 1670–1870.* Winnipeg: Watson and Dwyer, 1980.

Vines, Robert A. *Trees of East Texas.* Austin: University of Texas Press, 1977.

———. *Trees of North Texas.* Austin: University of Texas Press, 1982.

Vogel, Virgil. *American Indian Medicine.* Norman: University of Oklahoma Press, 1970.

Wallace, Ernest, and E. Adamson Hoebel. *The Comanches: Lords of the South Plains.* Norman: University of Oklahoma Press, 1952.

Warren, Harris Gaylord. *The Sword Was Their Passport: A History of American Filibustering in the Mexican Revolution.* Baton Rouge: Louisiana State University Press, 1943.

Webb, Clarence. *The Belcher Mound: A Stratified Caddoan Site in Caddo Parish, Louisiana.* Salt Lake City: Society for American Archaeology, 1959.

Webb, Walter Prescott. *The Great Plains.* Reprint ed., Lincoln: University of Nebraska Press, 1981.

Wedel, Mildred M. "The Ethnohistoric Approach to Plains Caddoan Origins." *Nebraska History* 60 (1979): 183–97.

Wedel, Waldo. "Native Astronomy and the Plains Caddoans." In Anthony F. Aveni, ed. *Native American Astronomy*, 131–46. Austin: University of Texas Press, 1977.

———. "Some Aspects of Human Ecology in the Central Plains." *American Anthropologist* 55 (1953): 409–513.

———. "Some Reflections on Plains Caddoan Origins." *Nebraska History* 60 (1979): 272–91.

Wheat, Carl I., comp. *1540–1861: Mapping the Trans-Mississippi West.* 2 vols. San Francisco: Institute of Historical Cartography, 1957–58.

Whittington, G. P., ed. "Dr. John Sibley of Natchitoches, 1757–1837." *Louisiana Historical Quarterly* 10 (October, 1927): 467–512.

Wood, W. Raymond. "Contrastive Features of Native North American Trade Systems." In *Oregon University Anthropological Papers* No. 4, 153–69. Eugene: Department of Anthropology, 1972.

Wright, A. W. "Tests Conducted on the Meteoric Iron of Texas." *American Journal of Science and Arts*, ser. 2, 11 (1876): 257.

Wright, Carl C. "The Mesquite Tree: From Nature's Boon to Aggressive Invader." *Southwestern Historical Quarterly* 69 (1965): 38–43.

Index